Alicia and Kit Kenyon are stunned to discover that their recently deceased brother has gambled away their family home. They find themselves tenants of Major Andrew Harbury, a man who both puzzles and provokes Alicia. Kit, on the other hand, is determined to regain Herringham, but his wild schemes lead him to the brink of treason. The Major claims to be an intelligence agent, but is he on the side of England or France? Clearly he is involved in some intrigue, so how can Alicia trust a stranger when her own brother is suspected of dallying with the enemy across the Channel?

# Master of Herringham

## Julia Murray

**MILLS & BOON LIMITED**
London · Sydney · Toronto

First published in Great Britain 1979
by Robert Hale Limited, Clerkenwell House,
Clerkenwell Green, London EC1R 0HT

Australian copyright 1982
Philippine copyright 1982

This edition published 1982
by Mills & Boon Limited, 15–16 Brook's Mews,
London W1A 1DR

ISBN 0 263 73861 2

04/0582/

Set in 10 on 11½ pt Linotron Times

Photoset by Rowland Phototypesetting Ltd
Bury St Edmunds, Suffolk
Made and printed in Great Britain by
Cox & Wyman Ltd, Reading

# CHAPTER
# ONE

THERE was a stunned silence. Of the four people in the room only one seemed at his ease, a tall man, dressed in the gleaming top-boots and well-cut tail-coat of the fashionable man of 1813, seated rather out of the way at the back of the wide green drawing-room. Miss Alicia Kenyon, a young woman in her early twenties, and dressed in a gown of black crepe that ill became her fair complexion, stared in disbelief at the lawyer, and from him in a kind of fascinated horror at the man at the back of the room. The will had contained no surprises. Indeed, Alicia had barely listened to the monotonous recital, knowing that the estate would be left in its entirety to her young brother Christopher, the fourth occupant of the room. A tall young man, he had been lounging rather carelessly by the window, his attention divided almost equally between the reading of his brother's will and the activity of the heron on the lake. But now his attention was wholly fixed upon the little lawyer, a frown puckering the smoothness of his youthful brow.

'Avery, what are you telling us? That Herringham is not mine?'

Mr Avery shook his bald red head. 'Unfortunately, Master Christopher, it seems that a few hours before his death your brother was involved in a game of hazard, at which he lost heavily. In order to remain in the game he

was forced to sell the deeds to his house to the Major.'
Here he nodded at the quiet figure. 'Doubtless he
intended to re-purchase very quickly, when his luck
turned, but unhappily it was not to be.'

'But—is it legal? Is there nothing we can do?' Disbelief was writ large across the young man's face.

'I regret nothing. Major Harbury's claim is perfectly
genuine. The house, together with the grounds, has
been his property since a few hours before your
brother's death. It is purely through a sense of delicacy
and consideration that he has not asserted his claim
previously.'

'This is preposterous.' Alicia Kenyon found her voice
at last. 'How do we know what this man says is true? We
have only his word!'

'Alas, Miss Kenyon, that is not so. There were witnes-
ses, my dear, reputable men. The deed of sale was drawn
up before a number of respectable persons. There is
nothing you can do.'

'Very well,' Alicia said calmly. 'But what of the money
my brother received? May we not re-purchase Herringham?'

The little lawyer removed his eyeglass and polished it
with his handkerchief. 'I regret, Miss Kenyon, that but
for a small amount your brother had invested in the
Funds there is no money. Mr Kenyon continued playing,
and continued to lose.'

'Are you telling us we are paupers, Mr Avery?'

'Well, now, Miss Kenyon, you are not paupers, precisely. There is your mother's money, still intact, I
believe, and your own fortune, of course.'

'I see.' Alicia's fortune, left to her by her father,
totalled barely three thousand pounds. 'I am grateful to
you for breaking it so gently. Perhaps, if we might
trespass on your good nature, you might find us some-

where to live, as far from here as possible, and within the shortest possible time.'

'That, Miss Kenyon, will happily not be necessary.' The gentleman at the back of the room had moved at last, walking to the front of the drawing room and permitting Miss Kenyon her first clear view of him. The black eye-patch she had already noted and also that the coal-black hair was shot prematurely with grey. She had not previously observed the scar, a thin white line, that travelled across the gentleman's left cheek, from beneath the eye-patch to the corner of his mouth. The right side of his face was handsome, and his eye bright blue. He fixed the eye upon her now with an expression of sympathy. 'Mr Avery has omitted to inform you that the Dower House was not included in the sale.'

'The Dower House?' Alicia repeated stupidly. She had forgotten its existence.

'Indeed. I understand that it is in a state of some disrepair, but when that is remedied you may of course live there.'

With difficulty Alicia forced her mind to assimilate the facts thus presented. She had passed, in a matter of moments, from being possessed of a sizeable, if uncomfortable, residence, to being homeless, and now, propertied once more. 'If the Dower House is indeed ours perhaps it may be sold.'

'Naturally it may,' the lawyer concurred, smiling kindly on her. 'However, a house near your friends, in the area where everything is known to you—!'

Alicia met his eyes frankly. 'It is that that makes it objectionable. However, doubtless you are right. I daresay it would be foolishness to part with it.'

'I believe I should like to live there.' Kit's voice cut unexpectedly across her thoughts. 'The outlook is pleasant enough, Alicia, after all, and as Avery says we shall be near to all our friends! Where else should we go where we should not live like paupers?'

Alicia shook her head. 'I do not know. I find it so difficult—' She stopped, and brushed one hand quickly across her brow as though to push away dark thoughts. She forced herself to look up at the Major, standing over her. 'I daresay you wish us at the devil!' she said, with a feeble smile. 'If you will permit, Kit and I shall pack a few night things. The "Fox and Goose" will doubtless make us comfortable.'

'By no means! Miss Kenyon, you must remain here, I could not sleep easily thinking of you at a common hostelry.'

Alicia hesitated. The idea was attractive, she had to admit it, but then—She glanced doubtfully at the Major. Who was this man? 'Well, perhaps it will be easier. But only for tonight, of course!'

Andrew Harbury bowed. 'You honour me.' He turned to confront the little lawyer. 'Mr Avery, you will naturally not wish to journey back to London tonight. I shall instruct my butler to have a room prepared.'

It seemed this was too much for Kit. With a muffled expletive he swung himself away, bumping awkwardly into a spindle-chair which crashed onto its side, and wrenched open the door.

Alicia, startled, exclaimed: 'Oh dear! Gentlemen, if you will forgive me—' She did not wait for their answer, but turned as she spoke, and hurried through the door after her young brother. The Major watched her go, and then turned to the little lawyer with an expression of concern.

'It would seem our young friend is a trifle vexed with this business.'

The lawyer shook his bald head. 'Indeed, indeed! Most unfortunate.' He glanced briefly at the Major, and then polished his eye-glass consciously. 'Undoubtedly it will be an awkward time for them. Miss Alicia, you know, is a very determined young lady, not at all like her brother, her elder brother, I should say.'

The Major grunted. In his experience the deceased Mr Kenyon had been entirely worthless, but he hesitated to say so.

'Master Kit too,' the little man continued, 'is a very intelligent boy. His brother's death has affected him badly, I fear.'

The Major muttered something appropriate, and waited for this red-faced individual to come to the point.

'It occurs to me, my dear sir, although not at once, of course, no indeed—but after a little while, say in a few months—you might be persuaded to part with Herringham. I do not know what you paid, of course—'

'A great deal more than it is worth, from what I have observed,' the Major said, eyeing the unhappy lawyer grimly.

'Yes, yes, of course, but a man in your position—I mean, this house means nought to you. As you say it is in poor condition—'

'It is falling down, Mr Avery.'

'Yes, yes, of course it is! As I say, it means nothing to you, but to Master Christopher, and Miss Kenyon too, of course, it signifies a very great deal! If I might suggest—'

The Major's smile silenced him. 'You have already suggested it, I believe. However, I must request that you do not foster such hopes with these children. I have no intention of parting with Herringham. In fact, I intend to live here, and set it to rights.'

Mr Avery made no reply, but stared unhappily down at the papers he had strewn across what was now Major Harbury's desk.

'Besides which,' the Major continued, 'how do you suppose they could contrive to repurchase? You do not know what I paid, but let me assure you, I was content to accept Kenyon's evaluation of the property, which, it transpires, is vastly in excess of its true worth.'

'Yes, yes, but—'

'In addition to that,' the Major continued, fixing his eye with some sternness upon the little lawyer, 'how do you suppose they would contrive to maintain this barracks? From what I ascertain Kenyon was utterly scorched. Or perhaps there is something I do not know?' He looked in inquiry at the little man but he shook his head. 'In that case what did you intend? That I should make them a present of the house?'

Since this was precisely what Mr Avery had had in mind, although he had merely considered it as the return of what was rightfully theirs, he was quite unable to answer, merely flushing to an even deeper red than previously.

The Major smiled slightly, the scar puckering his cheek. 'An admirable scheme, purely altruistic, put into your mind, no doubt, by my foolishness over the Dower House. But I have, I think, already satisfied any such requirements by relinquishing all claim to that edifice. Do you intend that I should do the same with Herringham? How could I do such a thing? It would be the ruin of them, you know it. You know too that Kenyon, gambling as he was, would have been obliged to part with the house in any case. And I take leave to doubt whether he would ever have had the wherewithal to repurchase, always assuming that I had been prepared to sell.'

Mr Avery seemed confounded, and began with an embarrassed air to gather together his papers. He wished he had never attempted such a hopeless course.

Alicia Kenyon found her brother in his chamber. He had dragged a small, battered valise from the closet and was now engaged in ramming indiscriminately shirts and cravats into its interior. For a moment or two Alicia observed him, bemused, and then she said, in a bewildered tone: 'Dearest! What in heaven's name are you about?'

He glanced up, but did not stop his task, saying angrily: 'I am going to the "Fox and Goose", Ally, of course! What else should we do? I cannot conceive what you were thinking of in accepting that man's hospitality!'

'But Kit, this is madness! What else could I do? I own, I cannot like it, but it is excessively kind of him, after all! And you know,' she added fairly, 'the "Fox and Goose" is horridly dirty, besides being run by that dreadful Jedd.'

Kit flung her an irritated glance, and moved to pull a pair of hessians from the closet. 'That's quite nonsensical, as well you know! I'm surprised you even considered staying! Ally, we know nothing about the fellow!'

'I know, dearest, but I beg you will see reason! What sense is there in this hasty departure? Please, Kit, for me, do cease this foolishness!'

He stopped now, and regarded her frowningly. 'Ally, how can you wish to stay here? To see that fellow in our father's library? I wonder you can bear it!'

She sighed. 'I know, it is hard, but what can we do? Herringham is his, now, and we must accept it.'

'Well, I shall not,' Kit said forcefully, striding across the room as though he knew not what he was doing. 'What right has he to Herringham?'

'Every right! Gary needed the money, Kit, so he sold the estate. It is as simple as that!'

'Perhaps, if he will tell us how much it is worth, we might be able to buy it back.'

'Oh Kit, dearest, you do not know what you are saying! I wish we could! But besides the money, we could not afford to keep up the estate. There are the debts! When those are added, what hope can we have of repaying him?'

Kit glanced sideways at her. 'There might be a chance. There is something, anyway.'

His tone was such that Alicia began to be seriously alarmed. 'Kit, what do you mean? What have you done?'

He smiled at her. 'Nothing, love, nothing. 'Tis merely an idea.' He contemplated the scattered clothes on the bed, some pushed untidily into the inadequate valise, and sighed. 'I daresay you are in the right. It would be quite ridiculous, would it not, to stay at the "Fox and Goose".'

'Idiotish, love, indeed!' She smiled warmly at him. 'Kit, I know it is hard. I feel it myself, but we shall come about, you know. After all, it is not as though we are perfectly homeless.'

'No,' he agreed, smiling with an effort. 'We are not that.'

With her anxiety very little allayed Alicia left her brother's room to seek out the housekeeper. It occurred to her that something of what had happened should be conveyed to the servants, lest they refuse to accept the orders of their new master. She was anxious, too, that no garbled or improbable tale should be spread along those mysterious channels that always bore the news to the servants' hall. It soon became apparent, however, that something of the news had already been heard, for, passing through the green baize door she encountered a sniffing housemaid who peered at her through tear-blinded eyes. Realising after a moment who it was she bobbed hurriedly and set up a fresh fit of crying. Her heart sinking, Alicia knocked on Mrs Carter's door. It was as she expected. Within were Mrs Carter, also tearful, and her bracket-faced old nurse, sternly admonishing the older woman for her silliness. She turned on Alicia's entry, and the young woman realised, with a jerk of surprise, that her nurse was as indignant and upset as Mrs Carter, although her attitude was one of fierce and outraged loyalty. Already emotionally wearied, Alicia was obliged to listen to Nurse's homily, gathering at the end of it that she and Mrs Carter had no intention of remaining any longer under that roof, and if Miss Alicia were setting up her own establishment they would be happy to join her.

Alicia smiled. 'I don't know what you have heard about Major Harbury,' she said calmly, 'but I'm sure he is perfectly amiable! And I daresay it will be a very good thing for Herringham after all, for he is not without means, you know, and I daresay means to set it all to rights. Which,' she added candidly, 'you cannot deny it is in need of.'

Nurse Jeakes could not deny it, but, she said, she had served a Kenyon since first entering service, as had her parents before her and her husband also, now sadly departed. 'And serving upstart young men who know no better than to be stealing other people's homes is what I cannot do with,' she told her roundly. 'And if he's a Major why isn't he away fighting that dreadful Boneyparte like the honourable gentleman you say he is?'

'As to that, Jerry, I believe he may well have seen action. He is not uninjured, you know.'

'Huh, took a ball, did he?'

'A sabre slash, if I'm any judge, across his face. It cost him an eye.'

At this the wet-faced Mrs Carter exclaimed, but was frowned down by the more sternly-made Nurse Jeakes.

'Well, that's as maybe. But what do we know of him, Miss Alicia, tell me that.'

Since Alicia knew nothing at all there was little she could say, other than that she was sure he was a gentleman, and would not use them ill.

'Humph,' said Nurse, ignoring a fresh burst of weeping from the abundant form beside her. 'That's as maybe. But where's he going to sleep, that's what I'd like to know. Not the Master's room, that's for certain!'

Alicia repressed a smile. 'There is no reason why not, you know, seeing he is master now. However, I daresay when he sees the chamber he will decide against it. I'm sure it must be the gloomiest and most depressing chamber in the whole house!'

Nurse Jeakes gave her a quelling look. 'It is full of Mr Gareth's things,' she said, plainly shocked that Miss Alicia should speak so lightly of her departed brother's favourite room.

'Of course.' Alicia was quick to sense the disapproval. 'You are quite right, it would hardly be fitting. I daresay the blue room would be more suitable.' She rose to leave, but at the doorway turned and said: 'Prepare the pink bedchamber also, please, Mrs Carter. Mr Avery is staying tonight. We shall dine at six.'

She left them then, feeling some scruples as she shut the door about this high-handed ordering of what were, after all, no longer her servants, but a very short reflection convinced her that, as long as she remained in the house, by continuing as hostess she would be assisting rather than interfering, by assuming this role.

There had been a Kenyon at Herringham for nearly three hundred years. Edward Kenyon, gentleman, had chosen the site for his sixteen-year-old bride, and upon the rolling hills of Sussex had chosen to erect his large, awesome, and draughty Tudor mansion. Since that time

successive Kenyons had modified and added to the
original Hall, but it was an impression of Tudor grandeur that one received on turning through the lodge
gates. Inside one was greeted by a sweeping oak stair-
case, elegantly carved, that bore one to the upper
storeys. There were discovered dim and draughty passages, the intricate convolutions of which had served to
confuse many a stranger. Alicia, however, moved without noticing her surroundings, unerringly avoiding the
rotten floor-board at the top of the stairs, and walking
without hesitation down long passages along which no
natural light could filter. She gained her chamber in a
brown study, a frown puckering her brow, the fine grey
eyes heavy and anxious. Absently shutting the door she
moved to the window and peered through its leaded
panes at the gardens below. They were in a sorry state.
Since old Bakewell had died the year before there had
been no one to tend them, and cheerful flower borders
were now almost indistinguishable from the rank grass
of the South lawn. To be sure, in his last years Bakewell
had done little more than keep the immediate gardens
tidy and tend to his pride, the rose garden. Now, however, without even his guidance the bushes had thrown out
long, unkempt branches, and suckers drained away their
very life-blood. She wondered what the Major had
thought when the first impression of splendour had given
way to one of collapsing roof, crumbling stonework, and
rotten, worm-eaten wood. With a tiny shake of her head
Alicia turned away from this depressing aspect and
moved to pull the fraying bell-rope, noticing as she did
so that it would not be very long before it came away in
her hand.

Her summons produced, after a few minutes, the
spare form of her former nurse, who had taken upon
herself the task of attending her old charge when Miss

Alicia's abigail had left her service. 'And far better you'll be without that niminy-piminy creature,' she had told Miss Kenyon when she had bewailed her attendant's departure. 'A perfect wet-goose, she was, besides having no loyalty to the family. So don't you worrit yourself, Miss Alicia, for I can serve you quite as well as any stuck-up widgeon from London, and that's a fact.'

So Alicia had smiled and given way, perfectly willing to submit once more to the autocratic rule of her gruff, kind-hearted old nurse.

She entered now with her lips primly folded, an expression on her face of one who could, if questioned, say a very great deal on the subject, but who would not, otherwise, so demean herself. Alicia smiled slightly.

'Jerry, I am in such a hobble! Do tell me! What shall I wear tonight, do you think? I have only this one black dress, until that muslin arrives from Brighton, and shall not, for all the world, appear in it again for dinner! The Major will think us quite run off our legs if I do so, and, for all it is the truth, I do not care so to display it! So tell me, do you think it would be vastly improper, dearest Jerry, if I wore my grey cashmere?'

Nurse Jeakes sniffed. It was, to be sure, a knotty problem, but after a moment or two's reflection she smiled sourly and patted her charge's hand. 'No, Miss Alicia. I do not think Master Christopher would object, and as for the Major, well he has no right to think anything at all! Besides,' she added, with the tone of one delivering a clincher, 'it is by far the most becoming dress you have, if I might be permitted to say so.'

Nurse Jeakes was permitted by her unexacting mistress to say more or less what she wished, as she well knew, but nevertheless Alicia smiled and planted a quick kiss on the older woman's shrivelled cheek. 'Thank you, Jerry, that is precisely what I wanted to hear! So, since I have not worn it this age perhaps you could find it for me, dear Jerry, and see it is in some order for me to wear? I think I shall just rest on my bed for a half hour. I feel fagged quite to death!'

Divested of her black gown Alicia lay back on the bed, permitting her nurse to ensure she was safely stowed before she sniffed once again and withdrew. Alicia sighed and closed her eyes. Since Gareth's death a week before she had slept but fitfully, and today, with the strains of the afternoon, she was sure she would soon be fast asleep. It was not to be, however. The anxieties that had beset her upon her brother's death seemed now larger than ever, and in spite of her exhaustion, served to keep her in a state of tension. She gave little thought to their future; she supposed vaguely that they could stay with their Aunt Mary until the Dower House was fit for habitation. It was her younger brother who occupied the major part of her thoughts. His behaviour that afternoon had been the culmination of several weeks' strangeness, since a time long before Gareth's death. Over the past six months he had become more and more preoccupied, his temper less even, and altogether less patient with herself and the servants. To the steady Kit it was a great contrast, and Alicia could not but be worried.

For the past four years Kit had been in almost sole control of the estate. Their mother's death had driven Gareth from them, to a life of excess and self gratification in the metropolis. He had visited them less and less, so obviously preferring, even in summer, the pleasures of London to the responsibilities of a landlord that Kit had long since ceased to bother him about estate matters, taking more and more responsibility onto himself until, at the age of twenty-one, he assumed formally the position of his brother's steward. Still only twenty-two,

he had proved himself a worthy substitute, and although
Gareth was occasionally concerned by the long, complicated letters his clever young brother wrote concerning
the state of affairs at home he did not scruple to draw
indefatigably on the estate for his immediate needs in
town. To Alicia Kit communicated little of his troubles.
It was plain to her that the house was in bad order, that
the efficiency of the home farm had fallen off vastly of
late, and that those servants who had chosen to seek
greener pastures had never been replaced. They were
operating now on a skeleton staff. Between them Keen,
the butler, and Mrs Carter, virtually ran the house. A
few maids had been retained to help with menial tasks,
and there was a boy, Tom, who looked after the stables.
Herringham was but a shadow of itself. The once magni-
ficent library had been reduced to those few volumes
that were Kit and Alicia's personal property—Gareth
was not bookish—and pale squares on the walls gave
testimony to departed paintings. Most of these, Alicia
knew, had been sold to pay her brother's gambling
debts—he seemed to divide his time almost equally
between games of chance, and visits to Newmarket and
the Whitehall cockpit. Gareth's letters would consist
solely of demands for money—he rarely told them how
he did, and never inquired into their own state of health.
On his rare visits to the home of his ancestors he
occupied himself by assessing the worth of his various
possessions, and, on his final visit, had infuriated his
sister by removing the silver epergne from its position on
the dining table—to be cleaned, he said, by a bang-up
London silversmith. Representations had had no effect.
When told of the effect of his actions he had merely
shrugged, a frown corrugating the perfection of his
noble brow, and recommended her to refer such matters
to his clever young brother who was, he said, so much

more up to snuff than he. The truth of this remark was only too evident. Gareth had inherited not only his father's features—in appearance he was an Apollo—but his mental capacities and incurable passion for gambling. Edward Kenyon, indeed, had given his son little to look up to. Having started the decline of the family fortunes by his disastrous luck at piquet and other games of chance he had succeeded in drinking himself to death by the age of forty-five. Gareth, inheriting at nineteen, had suffered the tutelage of a fusty collection of trustees until reaching his majority, and then, with a smile at his frustrated Mama, had dispensed with all advice that could tell him to do other than he wished.

His young brother's flair for management he had seen as a blessing. While there was nothing Kit could do without the master's express permission, he kept things running smoothly, retaining for Gareth valuable tenants, and seeing where corners could be cut without endangering the success of the whole venture. Graciously granting his young brother formal stewardship he had virtually washed his hands of Herringham, regarding it merely as a very welcome source of funds whenever he found himself in Dun Territory.

Alicia was not surprised he had sold the house. He had had little affection for any of them, excepting perhaps Mama, and none at all of the love for the house that Christopher Kenyon possessed. She merely marvelled that he had thought to provide for them at all, by retaining the Dower House. She wondered that Kit had been so ready to live there. She had expected that he, like her, would have wished to be as far away as possible, and yet he had shown himself anxious to remain within very sight of it. To be sure, he had been reluctant to remain that night, had indeed been quite vociferous on the subject—strange for her steady, equable Kit. No doubt he was still in shock. Indeed, Gareth's death had affected neither of them so much as had the sale of the house.

A soft scratching at the door put an end to this reverie. Realising that the half-hour must be up she sighed, and, swinging her feet to the floor she called to her nurse to come in.

The meal that followed was a constrained affair. Since the departure eighteen months previously of the French chef Mrs Carter had undertaken the cuisine, and her skill with capons was not to be envied. Mr Avery, sensing the atmosphere, did his best to make light conversation, but, although assisted by the Major and Miss Kenyon, there seemed to be little safe or indeed common ground, and the silence of Christopher Kenyon served to throw the whole company into a fit of the dismals.

For his part the Major was glad of the opportunity to observe the young man. The tension was obvious, for although he kept his eyes largely lowered to his plate he was yet clearly conscious of the older man's presence, starting when the Major addressed him and darting quick, anxious glances at him from across the table. The Major sighed. His task was going to be harder than he had foreseen, for he had been quite unprepared for such fierce loyalty, and indeed, the presence of Miss Kenyon afforded an added complication. The spinster sister had certainly been mentioned; what he had not expected was a spirited young woman of perhaps four and twenty, with fine, intelligent grey eyes, and a very determined chin. He watched her now as she conversed in a constrained manner with Mr Avery, noticing with appreciation the delicate flush across the high cheekbones and how her eyes took fire when she was animated. She had exchanged that appalling black crepe dress for one of a fine cashmere, grey, and made high to the throat with a row of small buttons. It was quite plain, as befitted her bereaved state, but served to show rather more of her shape than had that outmoded gown of the afternoon. She was a brunette, unfortunately, but nevertheless not to be despised.

Conscious of his regard Alicia took care not to look at him. There was something about his presence she found disturbing, and which was not wholly explained by his somewhat sinister aspect. This, she felt, could be attributed largely to the black eye patch, and to the thin scar that gleamed white against his dark skin. But his remaining eye, she had noticed early, was possessed of a strange light and glitter that could change disconcertingly to an amused and tolerant twinkle. Without realising it she raised her eyes to his face, contemplating him gravely as she drained her glass. He was certainly well-looking, there was no denying it, even though there was a dark ring beneath his eye and he looked as though he had not slept well in some little time. The white scar gave his face a permanent, half-mocking look the way it pulled his mouth upwards at the corner. Except when he smiled, of course. Even Miss Kenyon was not proof against a handsome smile, and several times during that indifferent meal in spite of her troubles had she found herself responding in like fashion. It irritated her, for she had determined to display a frosty coolness, hoping to put this interloper in his place. But he would not be perturbed. Her coldest replies were met with that twinkling look and a smile that made her think, extraordinary though it was, that he was not indifferent to her plight. The arrival of the port made her start, and she rose somewhat hastily. As she was about to quit the room, however, the Major addressed her, requesting that he might have speech with her at some later hour in a room of her choosing. Kit's eyes flickered upwards at this request and it seemed for a moment as though he would speak. Apparently he thought better of it, merely stretching his hand for the crystal decanter. Alicia responded that provided he did not mind she would be in her mother's sitting room, which he would find opposite the drawing room.

When she had departed Kit raised fiery eyes again to demand in a scarcely controlled voice what business he could have with his sister.

The Major surveyed him coolly. 'I wish to discuss certain matters with her of a domestic nature,' he responded calmly. 'You may of course be present an you choose. We shall not be talking secrets.'

Kit's eyes blazed. 'Would that you had never come here!' he cried explosively, pushing his chair back so violently that it fell with a crash to the ground. 'What is Herringham to you? Why could you not leave us alone?'

'To do what, bantam?'

'To . . . to live our lives as we choose! We did very well until you forced yourself upon us!'

The Major smiled slightly, infuriating the young man. 'Were it not I it would have been someone else, sure as check. Nothing is more certain than that Kenyon would have sold his house. Even you must see that.'

Speechless with rage Kit confronted the older man across the table, his blazing grey eyes meeting that single intense blue one. Finally the gaze seemed to overawe him, for his eyes fell, and, turning, he stumbled over the fallen chair and almost ran to the door. His expression bland, Major Harbury caught up the decanter and casually refilled Mr Avery's glass.

Having seen Mr Avery conducted to his chamber Major Harbury walked frowningly along the dimly lit passage to Miss Kenyon's sitting room, the sound of his feet little dulled by the almost thread-bare carpet. Rotten and faded hangings covered the walls, making the passage darker even than was strictly necessary, and they would, he strongly suspected, disintegrate at a touch. He found Miss Kenyon apparently occupied in sorting some old papers, for these were spread across a substantial area of floor, and little piles had been created on the low table before the couch. She looked up as he entered, with a spontaneous smile.

'How quick you were!' she marvelled, laying down a pile she had been perusing on one side. 'In the general way the gentlemen take hours over their port, or so I am informed! We do not have a great many gentlemen visitors at Herringham now, unless you can count Uncle Henry, my mother's brother, and my cousin Gregory.'

'Your cousin?' The Major smiled pleasantly on her and shut the door.

She nodded. 'If you are a society man I daresay you know him. He would have us believe he is called Beau Kenyon, though how much truth there is in that statement is questionable.'

'I know of him,' the Major replied, seating himself in a low armchair at right angles to her, 'although I am no member of his particular set.'

'Well, I do not suppose you have missed anything important, although he would have it he is quite a Nonpareil, an Arbiter of Taste!'

Major Harbury's lips twitched at the derision in her voice, but he said merely: 'He is quite a Corinthian, certainly.'

She glanced at him quickly. 'You do not like him, I collect.'

'Ma'am, I know him little. He is a member of what you probably call The Dandy Set, and although, to be sure, I cannot abide untidiness in a man, such extreme fastidiousness is quite beyond my comprehension.'

'I know *exactly* how you feel!' Alicia responded warmly. 'He is forever worrying about creasing his tails, or the set of his coat, or some such thing! Indeed, I find it perfectly odious!'

The Major laughed. 'Does he visit you very often?'

'Oh no, merely when he is obliged to rusticate a little, and then only when there is nowhere else for him to go. He finds us very dull work, I am afraid. Kit thinks him wonderful, of course.'

'Indeed!'

'Oh yes. If you like, I could take you to the picture gallery in the morning. Somehow, Kit managed to retain most of our ancestors for us, and there is a likeness of Gregory, quite fair, I believe, taken some five years ago.'

'I should be very interested, Miss Kenyon. As a matter of fact, it was about the morning that I wished to speak to you.'

Alicia was scarlet. 'Forgive me! I must have been boring you quite dreadfully! I had forgot you wished to talk business matters with me.' She glanced at the untidiness before her, and said constrainedly: 'I have been tidying some of Mama's old papers, I don't know how it is, but I have never tackled them before. They are largely collections of old accounts, but there is the occasional letter, and it seems unfair in me to leave such a task to you.'

Irritated with himself Andrew said: 'It is about such things I wish to speak with you.' He paused, contemplating her. 'I cannot but think it vastly unfair in me to expect you to leave your home the instant I walk into it,' he said. 'There must be many matters for you to clear up, and since the Dower House will not be habitable for many weeks it seems unreasonable to expect you to stay all that time at the inn.'

The grey eyes regarded him steadily. 'I own, I daresay I should find the inn excessively uncomfortable, especially if I were forced to make a protracted stay. However, I had some thoughts of writing to my Aunt Mary, my father's only sister. She lives near Guildford, which is not so very far away.'

'Too far for a daily visit, however.' He paused, and contemplated her gravely. 'Miss Kenyon, it seems to me quite proper and suitable that you should remain at Herringham, at least until your affairs are settled. Would you consider it?'

'Oh no, I do not think so!'

'It would be a vast help, you know, to have you here! The servants resent me heartily, so I am sure if you are here things are far more likely to get done!'

She chuckled. 'Fair and far out, I am afraid, Major. As long as I am here you are likely to have every one of your orders referred to either Kit or me!'

He smiled. 'Perhaps so, but it seems to me that if you do not remain I shall have no servants!'

She gave a perfunctory smile, but said: 'I do not know, indeed! I do not think it would concern me to see changes at Herringham—indeed they are sorely needed!—but I fear the longer we stay the harder it will be for us! Oh dear! If only I had some advice!'

'Since my view is perfectly selfish I cannot give mine. But I will say that from here you may superintend the work at the Dower House in a way impossible from Guildford.'

She glanced at him worriedly, and away again. 'If only I knew what to say! If it were only I—! But there is Kit, and I fear to remain here will be perfectly dreadful for him.'

Andrew nodded slowly. 'I see. He is, of course, still much affected. He was your brother's steward, I collect.'

'Yes,' Alicia sighed, 'which is what makes it so much worse. He cared for our inheritance in a way neither Gareth nor I could, though it pains me to see it brought to such a pass.'

'He could be of great use to me, you know,' Andrew said, regarding her closely. 'I know little enough of estate management, and nothing at all about Herringham!'

'If only he might! But I think it would be quite useless to ask him. A few months ago he would not have hesitated, I am sure, but now—!'

'Now?'

She sighed. 'Now he is so changed I scarcely know him! He was always wont to be so . . . so steadfast, Major! Oh, he had his wild moments, like any young boy! I remember once he bought some lilac pantaloons in Brighton, and was quite convinced he was, as he told me, all the crack! Unfortunately Gregory chose that week to visit us, and did not scruple, I can assure you, to put my poor young brother in his place! I do not believe I have ever seen him so crestfallen! However,' she said, realising she was rambling again, 'there is little of that Kit left now! He is irritable—the slightest thing makes him fly into the bows! I hardly know what to say that will not offend him in some manner. It is very provoking! Though of course,' she added, seeming to consider such ramifications unsuitable to a stranger, 'he has had a great deal to bear. Gareth, you know, was most inconsiderate, and quite hopeless as a landlord!'

'I see.' The Major frowned. 'I was hoping he might be persuaded to show me around the estate, and perhaps to introduce me to the tenants. However, I see I was mistaken.

'If only he might be persuaded! But I fear he will be vastly put out if only I suggest it to him.' She sighed, and forced a smile to her lips. 'I must admit, to remain here would be so much easier for us! Aunt Mary is a dear, but she is rather a pea-goose, I'm afraid! I daresay a week or two would be well enough, but when you talk of months—! And then, too, these workmen are so dilatory nowadays! It really would be vastly helpful to be on hand. If only I might persuade him!'

Thinking he had said sufficient the Major rose and in a moment had taken his leave. Alicia returned rather abstractedly to her mother's papers, but her attention was far from with them, and within a moment or two had sat back in thought.

Kit was in his chamber when his sister knocked, and the presence of a standish and paper on his little desk gave testimony to his occupation. Alicia noticed that the corner of a sheet of paper was protruding from the desk drawer, and wondered what he had been writing that needed to be so concealed.

'Why, Ally,' he said, breathing fast as though he had been running. 'Come in. How was your little talk? A delightful cose, I make no doubt!'

Her grey eyes sparkled, but she said merely: 'The Major is excessively kind. I daresay he wishes us at the devil.'

'As I do him! What is it with you, Ally, that he had so affected you?'

'Nothing. Indeed, I do not know that I like him above half. But it is true he might, an he wished, turn us away.'

Kit shrugged. 'I do not see that it signifies overmuch.'

'You might help him, Kit, an you chose.'

'I?' He laughed in amusement. 'What should I do for him? Has he not our house?'

'Yes,' she concurred, 'but he knows little about it.

However, I daresay he will learn soon enough.' She paused, and raised her eyes to his. 'He has offered us hospitality, Kit, until the Dower House is habitable. Should you not object I should like to accept.'

The grey eyes met, and then Kit shrugged. 'Do as you please. It signifies little to me where I am.'

Considerably surprised Alicia stared at him, and then, not desiring to press her luck, she bade him goodnight.

# CHAPTER
TWO

IT was a chill grey morning. The promise of rain was heavy in the air, the sky dark. Major Harbury stifled a sigh and urged his mount into a canter. He glanced thoughtfully upwards as a sharp breeze wafted the smell of rain towards him, and then put his head down into the wind. His destination was a small farmhouse some five miles inland. The directions he had been given were exact, including the tattoo he was to beat on the cheerful green door when he arrived. Chickens fluttered and squawked from the hooves of his horse as he rode gently across the yard. It was very neat, although the bad weather had created pools of water and muddy patches on the ground. Dismounting he led his horse to the stone trough and left the animal with its nose plunged gratefully into the icy water. Across the yard a black and white cat was watching intently at a hole in the wall, tail curled neatly round its toes. The Major considered it a moment then moved to give the prescribed knock on the brightly painted door.

A woman in a spotless cap, her face unbecomingly pink, opened the door. Her arms were floured almost to the elbow. She regarded the visitor for a moment out of sharp, fox-eyes, and then nodded and stood back from the door. The Major stepped directly into the kitchen, the heels of his boots clicking on the flagged floor. It was very hot. The oven doors stood open and a pile of steaming loaves had been set hastily on the scrubbed surface of the long wooden table.

'The sluggard's still a'bed,' the woman said shortly. 'Sit you down. I'll tell'm you'm 'ere.'

The Major drew out one roughly-fashioned wooden chair and sat down, laying one arm along the whitened table. One leg of the chair was shorter that the other three and it wobbled as he sat. The woman contemplated him frostily for a moment longer and then left the room.

The Major relaxed a little on his wobbly chair, stretching one booted leg before him. He could not see out of the square-paned windows for they were completely obscured by steam. The loaves beside him made him feel very hungry. Everything in the kitchen was spotless. Simple blue and white patterned plates were ranged along the high shelf above the ovens. Bunches of various herbs hung from the ceiling on hooks, all completely dried and ready for use. The Major felt his face growing scarlet in the heat of the room, and ran one finger round inside his neckcloth. He wished the fellow would hurry up.

As if on cue the door opened and a short, spare gentleman entered, his brown hair tousled, wearing a red brocade dressing-gown, sadly incongruous in the homely atmosphere of the kitchen. The lines of his pillow were impressed on one cheek and his eyes were still heavy with sleep. He nodded to the Major, whom he had never met before, and turned to the woman who was hovering behind him.

'I'll have a pot of coffee, if you please, in the front parlour.'

The woman frowned and seemed about to protest, then apparently thought the better of it and moved silently to where a kettle was boiling gently over the fire, adding its mite to the steam of the kitchen.

The gentleman stood with his hand on the handle of the door and indicated with a jerk of his head that the Major should follow him.

'Dashed surly female,' he remarked before they were out of her hearing. 'Excellent cook, though, so I suppose I mustn't complain.' He opened the door to another room and walked unceremoniously in. 'Well?' he said, turning to face his visitor. 'You have some news?'

Just over an hour later Major Harbury departed. The rain had not yet come, although the sky was darker even than before. His horse walked across the yard to meet him, blowing and nodding his head in greeting. The woman shut the door behind him without a word. Andrew shrugged, and, gathering the reins, swung himself easily into the saddle. The chickens flapped away as he trotted through them. In one corner of the yard, he noticed, the black and white cat was playing with a dead mouse.

Alicia Kenyon awoke to the familiar comforts of the room she had occupied since leaving the Herringham nursery some fourteen years previously. For a few seconds as she sat hugging her knees beneath the bedclothes she remembered nothing of the past ten days, that had begun with the news of Gareth's death, with Kit's journey to London to bring home the body, and had ended with his funeral and the reading of his will. With the clatter of her ill-fitting window came recollection, and as she swung her feet to the thinning carpet depression swept over her. Moving to the window she tried ineffectually for a moment or two to make it secure, but it would not fasten properly, and continued to rattle with the force of the wind. The day was grey and cloudy; the wind was blowing the barracks of the trees into a frenzied dance. Pulling the bell-rope she moved to her closet, and, rejecting at once the rusty black mourning gown of the day before she pulled forth a gown of grey merino, made high to the throat with a puritan white collar, and which, she had once said, made her look like a governess. When her old nurse arrived she was already divesting herself of her woollen night-gown and submitted with impatience to her attendant.

A guest in a house where she had once been mistress, Alicia felt awkward when her summons in the breakfast parlour produced no response. Mr Avery had departed early, and of the Major there was no sign, and besides, she decided she did not really feel very hungry.

In an effort to dispel her depression she moved on impulse from the gloomy room into the hall, and, pulling open the heavy front door, stepped out into the grey, chill morning. It was cold, but her gown was thick. She walked swiftly from the house, hurrying from the now sadly rutted drive into the ankle-deep grass of the south lawn. She knew where she would go, where she had always gone when troubled, or when desiring merely to be alone. Woods skirted the lawns, and with a splendid disregard for the welfare of her gown she gained these in a few minutes, exchanged dank grass for soft, decaying leaves, and, clutching her skirts tightly, headed up the wooded hill.

The fallen trunk had lain there many years. Alicia could still remember the night it had fallen, the great, ancient oak, that had stood so proudly, so alone, in a small clearing, crashing down in unwonted gales. Here she had come, in those years past, carried up the hill effortlessly, light as gossamer, cloud-borne, on those still, endless, glowing summer days of childhood. Here she had come, and here everything had been solved. Here, gazing out over the tops of the trees, over the uneven roofs of Herringham to the hill beyond, golden in the glow of sunlight, here, occasionally, for a long, breathless, suspended moment she had possessed the secret, known the answer, and the knowledge had flooded her, filling her very essence with wonder. Here she would stand, not daring to move, knowing the precious moment would be lost only too quickly. Then down she would run, dodging trunks, skipping the logs, arriving panting, laughing, fulfilled, on the grass again where her brothers would question her, and then, not understanding laugh at her.

Today it was the memory of that blissful communion that haunted her, the days when the future, unknown, but bright, and sparkling, lay untrodden before her. Now she shied from it, from the knowledge that if anything awaited her, bright and sparkling it would not be. Sitting on the bark-stripped and whitened trunk she forgot the chill of the air, the smell of rain in the wind, until drops of water were swept at her on a light, floating breeze from across the valley. Sighing, she rose, and started for the house, allowing the hill to pull her relentlessly downwards, to cast her, out of breath, on the lawn again, but without that wonderful sense of fulfilment of earlier years. Before the rain began in earnest she had gained the house, thrusting open the thick wooden door. With a little surprise she encountered Keen in the hall, and, conscious of her certainly dishevelled appearance, raised a hand to her hair, forgetful for a few seconds that this was Keen, who had known her from a baby, had seen her muddy-faced, tousled, dirty.

'Keen!' she said, breathless from running. 'Could you—is there any breakfast? I don't want to trouble you, but if Mrs Carter could manage something—' She hesitated, and then said: 'Has the Major eaten yet?'

'No, Miss Alicia,' responded Keen, 'but he went out early, I understand. I shall tell Mrs Carter to make breakfast. If I may say so, Miss, I believe she'll be more than pleased to oblige!'

Alicia smiled, and then laughed, feeling suddenly more comfortable, more surrounded by affection, than she had done for many years.

She dawdled over the simple meal, anxious to put off for as long as possible the moment when it would be necessary for her to return to the chamber that was no longer properly hers. At last she stood up, however, and was just crossing the cold, marbled hall when footsteps sounded down one of the many passages that stretched out from the focal point. Thinking it might be Keen she hesitated, turning in the direction of the rapidly approaching person.

It was not Keen. A moment later the Major appeared, apparently from the stables, for he was dressed for riding in top boots. These were now sadly muddied, and it did not take Miss Kenyon more than a second to realise that the new master of Herringham was soaked right through to his skin.

'Good gracious!' she exclaimed, stepping impulsively towards him. 'Have you been riding in this rain?'

A look of impatience had crossed his face as she approached him, but her words startled a laugh from him. 'I have indeed! You disapprove of my foolhardiness, I collect!'

'I do!' she answered him frankly, her eyes observing a trickle of water that ran from the hem of his coat into a puddle on the polished marble floor. 'Whatever possessed you to do such a thing?'

He smiled ruefully at her. 'My horse needed exercise, as I did, and besides, I was desirous of observing my new possessions.'

'I see! You were not greatly entertained by it, I should warrant!'

'No, Miss Kenyon, I cannot deceive you. When one groat was last fed into this estate I know not.'

'It has been a long time,' she agreed. 'My father began the decline, you know. In many ways Gareth was very like him.'

'Is there a picture of him also? You are to show me over the house today, do not forget!'

She smiled. 'I had not forgot, but you should change, sir, or you will die of a chill, and then where will we all be?'

He laughed, and moved to the stairs. At their head he turned again as though to speak. Then he smiled, and was gone.

His brow puckered in thought the Major walked slowly along the darkened passage to the perfectly adequate chamber he had been allotted on his arrival. He was a man of modest tastes, and Nurse Jeakes would have been grieved to have learned that he possessed no desire whatsoever to sleep in the master bedroom with its rotten hangings and sombre panelling, full as it was with ghosts of Kenyons past. He thought it likely that he would never find the need to exchange his room for one of such decaying grandeur.

He opened the door thoughtfully, not immediately perceiving the small, pinch-faced fellow then in the act of brushing down a coat of navy-blue superfine, one of his master's finer garments, fashioned some three years previously by Scott, when the Major had been on furlough.

Chegg glanced up from his task at his master and shook his head wearily. The Major presented a sorry sight, and Chegg saw plainly that many hours' work would be required on the Major's coat if it were to be returned to its former condition. Years of service had curbed his impetuous tongue, however, and he contented himself with an expressive sniff before laying aside the coat and moving to his master.

'And a lucky thing 'twill be if it don't settle on your lungs, sir,' the little man burst out, unable to control his feelings any longer. 'Fit enough y'are now but day'll come when you'll regret such doings as this, sure as check!'

The Major seemed to become aware of the little man for the first time and gave a perfunctory smile. 'Do what you can for the coat, though I dare swear it's ruined.'

Chegg sniffed, and silently helped his master from the well-fitting coat. He began fussing over it, and then, with a glance at his master's abstracted countenance, laid it aside. He had the greatest respect for his master, and knew that the work he was engaged upon was of the greatest importance. Some small idea of what it involved had been communicated to him when he volunteered his services, and if the Major, usually so cheerful, wore so grave an expression then bad indeed it must be. He lapsed into silence, therefore, merely assisting the gentleman from a shirt that seemed inclined to cling to his form.

'I hope the girl doesn't bring us to point non plus!' said Andrew suddenly, apparently following his own train of thought. 'She is too intelligent, Chegg, by far! I'll wager it's not long before she suspects the truth!'

The batman, who understood sufficient of his master's business for his words to be intelligible, nodded, and preserved a sympathetic silence.

'Now, I must rely on you,' the Major went on, allowing the man to help him into a clean shirt. 'She has promised to conduct me over the house. You must go through her chamber, Chegg, as carefully as you can. I cannot like it, but the slightest thing! She may, after all, be involved.'

'I'll lay wager she's not,' returned the batman gruffly.

'I hope not too, Chegg,' said the Major, giving him a wry smile, 'but 'tis better to know. The prettiest face can be a mask for deception.'

Chegg agreed, albeit reluctantly. 'Very well, sir, but I dunno what I s'll find.'

'Nothing, I hope! If you have opportunity to search the boy's room again do so. I may have missed something that you can see.'

The batman glanced uneasily at his master. 'And the other, sir?'

'Aye, the other! He exists, Chegg, of that I am sure! The boy is merely the pawn. Well, for him we can but wait. Now, Chegg, if you please, my cravat.'

Alicia awaited him in her sitting room, her occupation of the night before still apparent. She had made some progress, however, for the piles had been condensed into two only, and the waste-paper basket was full. As he entered she looked up with a smile and sat back from her work.

'Well, it is finished, as far as possible. I shall leave these letters for Kit to see, but the household accounts I'm sure he has no use for! Have you seen him, by the way?'

'Your brother? He breakfasted before me, I believe, and went out.'

'Oh.' Alicia appeared disconcerted. 'Well, never mind. Perhaps he has gone to look at our new home. I spould really do as much myself shortly, for I have not been inside for many months! My great aunt Margaret was used to live there until quite recently, but she was as scorched as the rest of us, and could never keep it in order.' She smiled to herself. 'She was the dearest creature, although she grew sadly deaf in the end, and took to carrying an ear-trumpet! But she was the drollest thing! She was quite a belle in her day, as you will see for yourself very shortly.'

'Where is she now?'

'Now? Oh, she died last year, of pneumonia. The Dower House was quite horridly damp, but she refused to quit it for the Hall. However, do not be sorry, for she was well over eighty and remained enormously cheerful until almost her last day.' She rose, and shook out her skirts. 'Are you ready? I do hope your man made you change your shirt, Major, or I am sure you will likewise be expiring of pneumonia!'

The Major smiled. 'Chegg takes quite good care of me, Miss Kenyon, you will be delighted to learn. In fact, I received a rare trimming for coming in in such a fashion. My coat, he informs me, is now quite ruined, and will take all his ingenuity to restore!'

She laughed, and moved through the open door. 'I'm sure you have a very good relationship with your man!'

'Oh indeed! He bullies me quite shamefully, but he has been with me since I joined the Army, and is quite awfully loyal.'

She looked curiously at him. 'Were you in the war?'

'Aye, Miss Kenyon! Where thought you I received this?' One finger touched his scar. 'I rarely duel, you know, and never with swords!'

She smiled, but blushed a little. 'Where were you?'

'In the Peninsular, for some little time. I received my wound at Aranjuez, on the Tagus river, and spent some weeks in the hospital at Alba de Tormes.'

He had spoken without emotion, but Alicia felt no desire for further information.

They had passed by this time into a different part of the house, along a route so confused that Andrew thought it unlikely he would find his way easily again. From time to time Alicia's gesture warned him of a rotten board, and once he was obliged to skirt a hole some twelve inches wide.

'My Uncle Henry did that, when he and Aunt Amelia were staying last year. He is quite portly, you understand, and like our good prince wears a Cumberland corset that creaks! I'm afraid it quite overset him. My cousin Gregory was here at the time, and he and Kit were obliged quite to drag him out!' She chuckled at the thought. 'Actually, Gregory was really rather offensive, he can be, you know, when he wishes, and now my Uncle and Aunt will only visit us when they are sure he is not here!'

'Your cousin has a cruel tongue, I collect.'

'Yes indeed! He is very clever, you know, and makes a point of discovering where one is most vulnerable. He can be quite witty when he chooses, but nearly always at someone's expense. Poor Uncle Henry is so sensitive about his size, though it is perfectly true he never makes the smallest shift to do anything about it, but there was really no need for Gregory to taunt him so, and call him—well—such things, to his face.'

'As fat as a flawn?' the Major suggested, his eye twinkling.

'Well, yes!' Alicia admitted, chuckling. 'But poor Uncle Henry was so put out, for he likes to pretend he really is not fat at all, which is the greatest piece of nonsense, of course, but still—!'

They had reached a pair of doors by this time and Alicia, laying her hand upon the brass handle, said over her shoulder: 'Here we are! You shall be obliged to wonder and marvel a very great deal, you know, and say we are a very handsome family, and appear vastly interested in what, I am sure, must seem the dullest work to you!'

She threw open the door now, and revealed another

dark gallery, illuminated at the far end by a long window with leaded panes.

'Not so full as you might expect, Major,' she said, glancing at him with a smile. 'We are quite a *new* family, you know. The first Kenyon to build here did so with his prize money. He was a Captain in Queen Elizabeth's navy, and grew quite adept at robbing Spaniards. Here he is. Gregory looks very like him, I always think. The eyes are so very shrewd, and alive.'

The Major studied the stylised portrait for a moment or two, assimilating the little pointed beard, and cunning, dark eyes.

'This poor creature was his wife. He married her at sixteen when he was well over forty. She bore him ten children, and was a perfect wet-goose, by all accounts.'

They proceeded up the gallery, observing Kenyons in long curled wigs and feathered hats, and then Kenyons with close-cut Puritan hair, the same dark, glittering eyes occurring again and again in the paintings.

'This is my Aunt Margaret. I told you of her earlier. She was used to live in the Dower House.' Alicia paused before the painting of a girl in a full dress with a very wide hoop, one slender hand drooping to where a greyhound stared lovingly up at her. She was very pretty, with laughing grey eyes.

'You look very like her,' Andrew remarked.

'I?' she laughed. 'Indeed, she would not have thanked you! She was one of the most sought after beauties of her day! Her hair is powdered, of course, but I believe it was quite corn-gold!'

'Not the hair, I warrant, but the eyes, and something in the curve of the mouth. Yes, certainly you have the look of her.'

Alicia blushed, and to cover her confusion moved on, saying briskly: 'Here is our family. See how like my father and Gareth are! Neither true Kenyons, with those blue eyes.' She moved on again, but the Major stopped to examine the little wide-eyed girl at her mother's skirts, and then smiled, and moved on. 'Here is Gregory, with Kit and me. You see how like old Edward he is? This was done a little while ago, of course, when I was sixteen. We are all in black, you notice, for my father had just died.' She paused a moment, and then pointed at a smaller picture. 'Here is my brother Gareth, also in black, you notice. Lawrence painted it. My brother commissioned them all. It was one of the first extravagances of his inheritance. I always wonder why Mama permitted it.'

Major Harbury glanced briefly at the smaller painting, wondering at the man's vanity, and then turned to study the picture of Alicia and Kit with Gregory, their cousin. Again the eyes, dark and mocking, glittered out at him.

'He can look quite wicked when he wishes, can he not!' Alicia remarked, noticing the direction of his attention. 'But then you know him, of course.'

'A little. We are not frequently in the same set.'

His tone was abstracted, and, glancing sharply at him, Alicia saw how closely he was observing the portrait. But he stood back now, and smiled at her. 'It is very true, I believe, of you. How unlike you and Kit your brother was.'

'Yes. We have the more aquiline cast of true Kenyons, Kit particularly.'

They had come to the end of the gallery by this time and Alicia moved to stare out of the long window. It was still raining, and she smiled ruefully at the Major as he came beside her. 'You are not seeing Herringham at its best, I fear! When the sun shines it can look very lovely. The stone glows, you know, so that sometimes it seems almost aflame.'

He was looking out into the garden, and now frowned. 'Someone has been tending these gardens. Those borders have been weeded recently.'

'Yes, I try to do a little. That one bed is all I ever manage. Foolish, really, when there is so much.' She pondered a moment. 'I daresay at the Dower House I shall be able to keep it quite tidy.' She turned now, and moved to a small door. 'We can get back to the hall this way. It is much quicker.'

He followed her down the narrow stone stairway, and in a shorter time than he would have thought possible they had arrived back in the entrance hall.

'There are a great many other chambers, of course, but they are all shut up, and indeed, I should not care to go into them until the floors are checked.' She hesitated, and then looked up into his scarred face. 'I think I shall walk over to the Dower House now it has stopped raining. Should you care to come? I should like to see it, and besides, I am a little worried about my brother.'

He consented, and she left him to fetch her wrap.

Kit had woken early that day. Like Alicia he had lain for a moment or two without recollection, and then he was up, and dressing himself with unwonted haste. The day before he had scarcely known what he was about. Today all seemed plain. The long night had brought good counsel, and he tore up the letter he had penned the night before. Calmer now, he wrote again, and, satisfied, dusted the single sheet. His first inclination had been to run as far as he could from the house, from the man who was now master. A little reflection, however, had shown him how unwise would be such a course. When Alicia had announced her intention of remaining at Herringham he had just decided that the only sensible course was for him to do just that. Consequently he had agreed, although not in a manner that might make his sister suspicious.

Emerging from his chamber he satisfied himself that no one, especially the Major, was about, and hurried down the stairs. There was no one in the stables when he arrived, so he hastily saddled his mare, and in a moment or two was trotting away down the drive. What he failed to see was the Major's batman, Chegg, who had followed him from the house, and who now observed his departure.

Little remained of Margaret Kenyon's garden. In her later years she had done little more than to get Bakewell to cut her grass, and perhaps to prune her roses once a year. Now the grass was as rank as that of the south lawn, and so long that it was with difficulty that the Major thrust open the wooden gate. It seemed plain to both that no one had entered for some little time.

The house itself was gracious, of a period with the Hall, but more elegant, and far less rambling. The door shuddered as the Major pushed it open, and a little shower of powdery wood gave signal of its rottenness. Their entrance produced a scurry of activity across the floor, and Alicia squealed and clutched the Major's arm as a tail disappeared into the wainscot.

'A rat!'

He smiled, 'No, a mouse, merely. Do not tell me you are not familiar with them! I daresay I have a family inhabiting my room! They almost kept me awake.'

'Oh, for shame!' she protested laughing. 'It is not *so* bad! I admit there are a few, but never enough to keep you awake!'

'I definitely heard chewing,' the Major insisted. 'I was quite worried for my boots.'

She laughed, but said: 'You know that is all a nonsense! Well, Kit is clearly not here, but perhaps we should look around anyway, for I fear there is a great deal to be done.'

This was apparent. Much of Margaret Kenyon's furniture remained, sombrely shrouded, and generously covered in dust and cobwebs.

'I had not realised how much of Aunt Maggie's remained,' Alicia remarked, lifting one corner to peer at the chair beneath. 'I daresay most of this is rotten also, for I do not believe a fire has been lit since last year. However, we might be able to save something.'

The Major was surveying the room, a drawing room, which must once have been very fine. The panelling made it a little dark, it was true, but nevertheless the Major thought that with a little care it might prove attractive.

'Possibly,' Alicia agreed, when he voiced his opinion. 'However, I daresay it is very wormeaten.'

The rest of the house proved equally depressing, and Alicia was glad to step once more into the tangled garden and breathe the fresh, rain-scented air.

'I shall be engaging a carpenter,' the Major said, 'to repair some of the floors at the Hall. If you choose, I shall engage one for you also.'

'Thank you! That is indeed kind.' She hesitated, and then said: 'Do you intend to live there, Major? Or have you other estates, perhaps?'

He smiled down at her. 'Being a younger son, Miss Kenyon, I have no other estates. I daresay I shall spend some months here. I certainly intend to make it viable again.'

'Well, if you do, I hope you are pretty plump in the pocket, for it will take quite a fortune, I fear, to do all that is needed!'

'I am aware, but fortunately, even though I am a younger son, I am pretty plump in the pocket!'

She sensed his laughter, and blushed. 'You wonder that I use cant phrases, I collect, but when one has brothers it is very easy to pick up their ways of speech!'

'Brothers are a sad trial,' Andrew agreed, solemnly. 'My own brother, Paul, found me the most tiresome young cub imaginable, I fear, some years ago! He was really sorely tried on my behalf.'

'That I can believe,' she answered frankly. 'Tell me, is he a gamester too?'

The lips twitched, but the Major said gravely: 'He is not, and I believe he has found my proclivities a sad trial! But to do him justice he would never betray me. I would always turn to Paul if I needed help.'

'Which is doubtless why he found you so tiresome,' she ventured, regarding him from beneath her lashes.

He chuckled. 'Oh undoubtedly. I was forever in some scrape. I remember the poor fellow had but just returned from Spain with a shoulder wound and I was on his doorstep pestering him for funds.'

'He was in Spain too?'

The Major nodded. 'He was wounded at Corunna. It finished his career.'

'What does he do now?' she inquired tentatively.

'Now? He is a man of leisure.'

'I suppose you must think it rude in me to ask all these questions, but you have been rather sprung on us, you know, and Kit and I being so removed from society we know nothing of you!'

He smiled. 'I am nothing remarkable, I assure you!'

'Perhaps not, only do tell me, are you related to the Lord Harbury my father knew?'

'What think you?' he asked her, the blue eyes quizzing. 'Do I look so very much the gentleman?'

'Well, of course you are the gentleman!' she retorted. 'That much is obvious!'

'Is it so?' he responded musingly. 'I wonder if it would interest you to know that my father was a highwayman?'

'A high—Oh, now you are quizzing me!'

He shook his head. 'I am perfectly serious, Miss Kenyon. My father, in fact, was very much an adventurer, as I am. He made his fortune on the High Toby, and at piquet.'

'Oh.' She appeared non-plussed. 'Really, Major, you are too provoking! How am I to know what to believe?'

He laughed. 'My sweet life, you may believe what you choose! Only do not think me a gentleman, for I assure you I am not!'

She looked at him consideringly, but he merely smiled and shook his head. She seemed unaware of the familiar way he had addressed her. 'Well, whatever you would have me believe you cannot deceive me into thinking you are not kind! You had no reason to offer us houseroom!'

He smiled wryly and said: 'Had I not! Mr Avery would believe I should have made you a present of the house!'

She was startled, and said in a mortified tone: 'I would he had not done that! Oh, I know he has our interests at heart, but it is a great deal too bad of him, indeed it is, so to trespass on your good nature!'

'Good nature!' The Major seemed amused. 'There are not many who think I possess that, except perhaps my mother, and she is biased, as are all mothers!'

Alicia smiled. 'Your mother still lives, I collect.'

'She does indeed, with my brother and his wife.'

They had passed by this time into the Park, and their attention was arrested by the sight of a solitary rider, about half a mile away, trotting gently up the main avenue towards the house. 'That must be my brother,' said Alicia, starting forward. The Major gathered that their outing was at an end, and they walked briskly up the narrow path towards the Hall.

# CHAPTER
# THREE

CHEGG sighed, and stretched himself in the chair, trying vainly to find a position more conducive to repose. He was beginning to wish he had, as his master had suggested, gone to his bed, but his custom was to see his master safely stowed, and nothing, least of all a tiredness in his brain and a stiffness in his limbs, was going to make him waver. All the same the chair he had selected for himself in his master's dressing room was regrettably hard. He was just wondering what he could do about this fact when a slight click from the corridor arrested his attention and he rose from his chair. Hurriedly extinguishing his candle he opened the door onto the darkened passage. There was no sound, but a crack of light came from beneath the door to Christopher Kenyon's dressing room. He frowned, and stationed himself so that he could see with ease along the passage through the smallest crack in the door.

Miss Alicia Kenyon was also wakeful. Indeed, she had much to occupy her mind, and it was not surprising that sleep should refuse to come. Although much of her mind was directed towards concern for her brother, more than half of it was considering the tall sinister person of Major Harbury, so simple, and yet so much of an enigma. Although grateful, she had taken his kindness so much for granted that it was not until she retired to bed that night that it occurred to her to wonder why the Major should so concern himself in their affairs. They were nothing to him, after all. Out of charity to them he had forborne to claim his property until after their brother's funeral, though she did think, now, that Mr Avery might have given them *some* warning. And now, when he must be wishing them at the very devil, he had invited them to stay for as long as they chose, even going so far as to engage a carpenter for them. But was that so very strange, after all? A naturally kind-hearted man would want to see that all was well with them, particularly when he had so recently deprived them of all they possessed.

Still she could not be comfortable. There had been the affair of the letters, her mother's letters, sorted the previous evening, and left in a neat pile on her dressing table with the tortoiseshell mirror on top of them to prevent their blowing away. When she had returned from the afternoon's excursion she had found them blown all over the room, littering the floor, as though someone had handled them, and then not been careful to place them just so beneath the mirror. But the Major had been with her all the afternoon, so was not the idea that her room had been searched totally ridiculous? No, as it transpired. Methodically she had gone through the room, and in more than one case had she found something not quite as she had left it. Unnoticeable, of course, had not some chance draught carried the pages of those letters all over the room. Perhaps it had been one of the maids, curious about her mistress. But a woman would have been careful to return the gowns to the wardrobe exactly as before, and certainly would not have allowed the sleeve of her yellow muslin to become so hopelessly creased. In vain did Alicia try to empty her mind of care. As she lay beneath the covers she found herself going over again and again the events of the past two days. Eventually it became quite obvious that she was not going to succeed in sleeping. Sighing, she sat up and drew back a little way the curtains that surrounded her bed. Nurse Jeakes had left the window curtains open as always, and with the glow of the fire Alicia could just distinguish the various items of furniture. Swinging her legs to the floor she fumbled on the nearby chest for candle and taper, and then padded barefoot across the floor. Thrusting the taper into the glowing embers of the fire she lit the candle, found her slippers, and with her wrap tossed about her shoulders walked to where she could just, in the flickering light of her candle, distinguish the door.

The passage outside was dark, but she knew it well, avoiding the heavy oak chest strategically placed to catch unawares anyone unacquainted with Herringham. The doors opening onto the passage were all bedrooms, and as she passed the one allotted to her mother she knew a slight pang for the days when she would undoubtedly have sought comfort on such a night in her mother's arms. The master bedroom adjoined it, and then followed the door to the adjoining dressing room. A little further down the passage was the door to the chamber used by Kit, and which should have been quite in darkness, since Kit had retired quite an hour before herself pleading a headache. It was in some surprise, therefore, that she observed a dim light filtering from beneath the door of the dressing room, and heard the unmistakable sound of a drawer being closed. She hesitated, and then as footsteps sounded within the chamber, quickly snuffed her candle and stepped back into the embrasure of the master dressing room. The door opened slowly and she heard someone sigh. Then the door closed, and as the man moved away she was able to distinguish quite clearly in the light of the candle that it was the tall figure of Andrew Harbury. Catching her breath she watched as he moved silently along the passage and turned to go down the wide stairway to the hall. Having allowed him a few seconds Alicia slipped from the doorway, and, using her fingers on the wall as a guide, crept along the now darkened passage to where she knew the stairs to be. The Major was in the hall now, and she saw him across the marble floor to enter the library. Not daring to think what she might find she crept down the stairs, her mind concentrating on the simple fact that he had left the library door ajar.

Stepping from the bottom stair onto the marble she was aware of a slight slap from her slipper, and hesitated for a moment, waiting for a reaction. There was none, so she crossed the hall to peer in at the convenient crack the Major had left.

He was alone. A fire burned inadequately in the hearth and he had drawn a large winged chair towards it to gain maximum warmth. He was unoccupied, leaning forward in the chair with his arms resting on his knees, but a decanter and a glass stood beside him on a low mahogany table, and a few scattered papers testified that at some time he had been reading. He had set the candle above him on the mantle shelf, and Alicia could see that although his face was expressionless it held heavy shadows, and the scar stood out white against his cheek.

Alicia was not aware of having made any sound but just then without turning his head he said quietly: 'Why do you not come in? It is cold in the hall.' He looked up now, and she saw one side of his mouth lift in a smile as his eyes met hers through the crack. Blushing fiercly she pushed the door open, and, forgetful of her garb, walked slowly towards him, her unlighted candle clasped tightly in one hand.

'What are you doing abroad at this time, I wonder?' he said, not rising from his seat. 'Spying on me, perhaps?'

His eye mocked her as she blushed again and came

closer to the fire. 'No, indeed!' she retorted, indignation rising at his words. 'I leave such things to you, sir!'

The smile flickered again, and she felt colour rising in her cheeks.

'I could not sleep,' she explained, lighting her candle from his, 'so I got up for a drink. I saw you come from Kit's room.'

She had expected to disturb him, but he seemed unabashed, merely smiling a little more warmly than before.

'Sit down,' he advised her kindly, 'and get warm. You could catch your death!'

She became aware of her garb, and was thankful for the thick, unbecoming nightgown Herringham draughts made essential in the winter. She pulled her wrap more closely about her shoulders, however, and having placed her candle next to his perched on the edge of a hard chair that stood adjacent to the fire.

He regarded her silently for a moment, and then said: 'You wonder doubtless what I was doing in your brother's room.'

'Of course,' she answered at once, 'have I not that right?'

'No,' he responded gently, 'since this is now my house. However,' he continued as she blushed for the third time, 'you have every right to be concerned for your brother's possessions. What can I say? You have found me out, so I must confess to a single fault. I have an incurable desire to know other people's business.'

She frowned, perplexed, for his tone was light and bantering. 'Sir, I wish you would not tease me so! Do you not know how concerned I am for Kit? Whatever you say about yourself you cannot disguise your kindness. I know that if you were in Kit's dressing-room tonight it was for a very good reason, and not merely, as you suggest, a desire to know other people's business.'

He smiled at her. 'Miss Kenyon,' he said gently, 'has it not occurred to you that it might be my business to pry into other people's affairs?'

'Your business?' she echoed, staring at him.

'Miss Kenyon, what would your reaction be if I told you I was an intelligence agent?'

She continued to stare for a moment or two longer, and then a delightful chuckle broke from her. 'Sir, what nonsense is this? Are you determined to make game of me? For if you are, I shall tell you to your head that you will cut no wheedles of that sort with me! I hope I am not such a slow-top!'

He grinned, but said: 'Madam, I should never make game of you! I have too much respect for your intelligence to do such a thing!'

She laughed uncertainly, wishing she could see him better. But the two candles, whilst illuminating her own features, served merely to throw the Major's further into obscurity. 'Very well, sir, I accept what you say, that you are a government agent. However, permit me to tell you that you will find no traitors here!'

He shook his head. 'Miss Kenyon, you place too much upon your estimation of my gentility! What makes you think I am a British agent?'

She smiled now. 'Why, that was indeed crack-brained of me! I should have seen at once that you are a veritable traitor!'

'You do not believe me!' the Major complained, shaking his head sadly.

She laughed. 'Of course I do not! Did you expect me to?'

'Of course. I should not lie to *you*.'

'What a bouncer that is!' she exclaimed indignantly, to

cover the embarrassment she had felt at such particular warmth.

He sighed. 'What can I say? If I tell you the truth you do not believe me!'

'If you told me the truth I should!' she countered swiftly, her eyes alight.

If she had hoped to discompose him she failed, for he replied smoothly, yet with amusement in his voice: 'How should you know it was the truth, Miss Kenyon, for such a slippery customer as I am?'

'A slippery customer! You are not that!'

He nodded sadly. 'It is too true, I fear! And a loose fish, too, if only the truth were known!'

'Oh, a *loose fish*! Now that I can believe!'

He laughed reluctantly. 'I am undone! A traitor you will not think me, but a loose fish you do not baulk at!'

'Of course not,' she told him roundly. 'Anyone can see that of you! I daresay you have a score of mistresses in your past!'

'Oh, at least a score,' he agreed cordially. 'However, you may be easy, for I never trifle with females of quality.'

'Well, I am glad of that, in any event!' she responded, a shade more sharply than she knew.

He smiled, and came to stand over her. 'I said, Miss Kenyon, that I never *trifle* with such ladies!'

Already cursing the hasty words that had betrayed the sense of pique she felt Alicia glanced up, considerably startled by the sincere note in his voice. But he was already moving away, and now, his back to her, was kicking life into the reluctant fire. At a loss to understand him Alicia said tentatively: 'Major?'

'You should go to bed,' he said shortly, trying to ignore the fact that she had risen and was standing close behind him. 'Your nurse will think you are become quite abandoned.'

His tone was harsh, and, bewildered for a moment only Alicia relaxed and smiled. 'Forgive me, Major, I was forgetting myself! With such a loose fish as you are it would indeed be imprudent in me to remain a moment longer!'

He hesitated a moment for some fit response, but he did not turn until she had nearly reached the door. Then, with a smile curling his mouth he said: 'You should not worry so much about such persons as I am! We were made to be adventurers!'

She smiled in turn, but said: 'You may tell me what you please, Major, but nothing will serve to convince me you are not a gentleman.' She waited a moment to see the smile return to that blue eye, and then she left him.

Chegg, standing in the shadows at the head of the stairs, was startled by the sudden appearance of Miss Kenyon. Pressing himself against the wall, however, he remained unseen while she passed, and then, having waited until Miss Kenyon's door clicked shut, made his way back to his position of watchfulness in his master's dressing-room. Downstairs in his library the Major stood pensive, furrows carved deep into his brow as he considered the interview. As he had expected his revelation had carried no weight with her, and he smiled a little as he thought of how she had reacted. The memory of Kit, however, drove all amusement from his face, and he turned from the fire in some impatience. He really found himself in a very difficult position. He had left by Mr Kenyon's dressing-room, it was true, but he had been in Kit's bedchamber, and how could he tell the young man's sister that not only was he not in his bedroom, but that for some reason all the bedclothes had been stripped from the bed. Seated in his library the Major had been awaiting the young man's return, his despondency caused by the suspicion that Christopher Kenyon knew some other way out of Herringham.

Kit had retired to his chamber with the intention of resting. He was sincerely exhausted—the strain of the past few months was telling on him—and besides the Major's company was not something he valued. So he had withdrawn, noticing his sister's look of concern, and had sought the sanctity of his bedchamber. This room of all those in the house, he now could feel comfortable in. Around him were the accumulated treasures of his short life; here he could shut away the world, including the Major and all he stood for. Dropping onto the bed he surveyed the familiar surroundings with a sense of relief, and was just about to pull off his boots with a jack when a scratching in the panelling arrested his action. In any other room he would have dismissed such a noise out of hand. In his bedchamber, however, it had quite another significance. Rising with alacrity he grasped a flickering candle and moved quickly to a section of oaken panelling beside the hearth. Feeling along the underside of the mantle-shelf he touched a hidden spring, and then stood back as one section of panelling slid behind another. Bent almost double in a space barely three feet high was a man, and he fell into the room as the panel slid away. Speechless, Kit watched as he staggered forward, and dropped with apparent exhaustion on the bed.

'What are you doing?' Kit demanded hoarsely when finally able to speak. 'You are four days early!'

The man, tall and lean with black hair and several days' growth on his chin, opened dark, glittering eyes and coldly surveyed his host. Then he sat up, and tapped his breast pocket.

'I could not wait. I was discovered.'

'But you are too early!' Kit told him desperately. 'It is not safe!'

Louis Gerande regarded him coldly, and said nothing.

'My brother is dead, but that is not the worst of it. It seems he sold the house to some Major before he died. The fellow's here now.'

The dark eyes glittered. 'Indeed!' There was no suspicion of accent in the Frenchman's voice. 'This is unexpected?'

'Of course!' Kit retorted, nettled. 'Do you think they would have permitted you to use this house had they known some soldier would be here to greet you? How was I to know my brother would die, having sold our house? It's not the act of a sane man!'

Gerande considered him. 'You are right, it is not well. However, we could kill him, I suppose. It is doubtful whether anyone would notice. A Major, you say.'

Kit nodded. 'Heaven knows why he should choose now, of all times. But look, you're not killing anyone!'

The man shrugged. 'What alternative is there? I can run no risks! I must get to France!'

'I shall get you there somehow,' the young man declared. 'I promised I would!'

'Indeed you did,' the Frenchman agreed.

'There is a way; I have already written, but you will have to wait here two or three days.'

The Frenchman drew breath. 'This I cannot do. They are behind me. You must arrange it.'

'I cannot!' Kit almost cried. 'The Major, he watches me so closely! And then there is my sister, she too, is suspicious! I rode into Herringham this morning for an hour or so and she fretted herself half to death! I cannot move without one or other of them watching me!'

The Frenchman continued to stare at him, his dark eyes strangely bright in the light of the candle.

'I have written to London. Someone will come, arrangements will be made. In the meantime you will have to go to the tunnel. It is the only way! I know it is unpleasant, but at least you will be safe down there, and there will be no boat before Friday!'

Still the Frenchman was silent, merely regarding the young man from beneath his brows.

'It's not my fault,' said Kit, reverting suddenly to the manner of a sulky schoolboy. 'I did not ask my brother to sell the wretched house! I shall bring you food, and . . . and drink, and you may have my bedding, or at least some of it! I don't know what else I can be expected to do!'

There was no answer, but the dark eyes were raised to his and the Frenchman regarded him coolly.

A slight chill at his heart Kit stammered: 'Are—are you hungry now? Shall I fetch you something?'

'Do so,' was the reply, and the eyes were lowered.

Having hesitated a moment Kit turned, and, thoughts jumbling in his brain, stumbled rather blindly into the corridor. For the first time he was thankful that Herringham possessed so few servants. He passed through the house and had gained the kitchens without seeing anybody. Once there he hesitated, not knowing his way about, but found his way eventually to the pantry and took cheese, and a lump of freshly baked bread. Mrs Carter would miss them, he knew, but he had always been a favourite with her and could simply say he was still hungry.

Back in his chamber the Frenchman accepted the offerings wordlessly, pulling apart the crusty bread and pushing it with little finesse into his mouth. Nervously Kit watched him, trying to curb his impatience, listening all the time for some tell-tale noise in the corridor. At last, after what seemed an age, Gerande had finished, and Kit rose from his chair.

'Why do you delay?' he demanded, as the Frenchman did not move. 'Someone could come at any moment!'

For a derisive moment Gerande looked at him, and then, rising, pulled the blankets and a pillow from the bed. Kit opened his mouth to protest, then thought better of it, and, catching up his candle, made sure Gerande was following him before bending into the passage. Inside was another spring, and when Gerande was inside Kit pressed it to slide the panel back into place. There was now no light in the passage save that from Kit's candle, and it flickered and fluttered feebly in the stale atmosphere. Kit was well-acquainted with the passage, however, walking swiftly with head bowed to a narrow spiral stairway. With one hand on the wall and the other grasping the candle he hurried surefooted down the stairs and into another passage at the foot. At the end of this was a door, and Kit carefully set the candle on the floor to retrieve on his return.

Glancing behind him he saw the shadowy figure of Gerande, and, his hand trembling slightly, twisted the old metal handle. The door opened inwards revealing a heavy curtain of creeper that hung down to conceal the door from the outside. Carefully the young man moved it to one side, rearranging it as best he might when they had passed through. They were now in what had once been an excellent vegetable garden, with a wall eight feet high around it. An arched door was set into the wall and through this they passed into an area once known as the shrubbery. Turning to the right they followed the high wall for several hundred yards, and eventually stopped. Kit had carefully covered the trap door when last he had used it, and now in haste he pulled away the stones and branches he had laid across it. It was a heavy wooden square laid into the ground with a large ring set

into the middle. It took both hands to raise it and throw
it back against the wall. Inside, narrow steps led downwards into the dark. Bent almost double, Kit descended,
pausing while Gerande pulled shut the door behind him.

There was now no light at all, but Kit did not hesitate,
standing up after a few more steps and counting carefully
so that he should know when he had reached the bottom.
Here was a lantern left, and Kit, fumbling a little in his
nervousness, finally managed to apply the light engen-
dered by the ancient tinder-box. The flame flickered
dimly against the rough stone walls, turning into di-
amonds the drops of moisture that hung there. After
about twenty yards the passage opened into a small
room. There was a rough table in the centre of the room
and on this Kit set the lantern, turning to confront the
man who had followed him so silently.

'I shall bring you food in the morning,' he said, 'but
you must remain here. Sure as check, if you come out
someone will see you, perhaps even my sister, and since
I know what you would do if that happened I prefer that
you should stay here.'

He waited for some sort of response, but Gerande
merely seated himself at the table and drew from his
breeches pocket a set of crumpled and dog-eared cards.
Watching for a moment Kit saw him begin to lay them
out, and then, despair in his heart, he turned, and made
his way back along the passage to the trap door.

'Oh.' Kit Kenyon stood uncertainly in the library doorway, his eyes on the casual figure stretched before his
father's desk. 'I'm sorry,' he said stiffly, 'I did not realise
you were here.'

He was about to close the door again when the Major,
who had glanced up when the door opened, said hastily:
'No, come in, please. I'd like to talk to you anyway.'

Kit hesitated a moment and then stepped into the room reluctantly and shut the door. 'What about?' he asked sullenly.

The Major smiled and stood up. 'You must resent me,' he said, moving towards the young man. 'I don't blame you, but you know, really it is not my fault. Anyway, I want you to know that you are welcome to stay here as long as you like.'

'Thank you,' returned the young man stiffly, 'but I do not anticipate the need to trespass long on your hospitality. As soon as the Dower House is in some order my sister and I shall leave.'

'As you wish.' The Major moved back to the desk and picked up a paper. 'I was wishing to employ a bailiff,' he said, not looking at Kit. 'There must have been one at one time. I was wondering if you knew if he was still in the district and wanting work.'

'I really could not tell you,' responded Kit ungraciously. 'Now, if you'll excuse me.'

'Of course,' replied the Major, smiling agreeably.

Of a sudden Kit was ashamed of his ill-humour. 'Staines was a good man,' he offered, keeping his eyes lowered. 'I daresay he still lives in the village.

'Thank you, Mr Kenyon,' said the Major. 'I shall set about finding him. I wonder, would you care to take some wine with me, or do you find it a little early?'

Kit considered, a frown puckering his brow. He regarded the Major thoughtfully for a moment, and then, with a little less of his former ill-humour said: 'Thank you. Shall I ring for Keen?'

'If you would.' The Major pushed his hands into his breeches pockets and wandered to the window to look out onto the garden. It was late afternoon, and the sun had broken through the clouds some minutes earlier. 'It must be sad for you to see the house thus,' he remarked conversationally. 'These gardens were obviously very fine.'

An impulsive response almost broke from Kit at the speech, but in time he recollected his intentions, and with an effort said: 'They were used to be beautiful. My father took pride in them. I tried to keep the estate going but Fortune was against me!' He laughed bitterly and turned from the window.

'I was hoping you might be able to tell me how they were used to be,' the Major said, turning to watch the boy as he paced the room. 'I know little enough of estate management. There must be little you don't know about Herringham.'

'Nothing,' responded Kit at once. 'But you will soon learn.' He sensed the older man's efforts to conciliate him, but was in no temper to meet him. He turned as the door opened to admit Keen, and it was with a fiery countenance that he realised how near he had been to ordering the old man.

'Wine,' said the Major, noticing and guessing the reason for Kit's confusion, 'and two glasses.'

'Did you know my brother?' Kit asked suddenly, swinging to face his host.

'A little,' responded the older man, smiling slightly.

'You played cards with him, I collect.'

The Major bowed.

'I hope you had better luck than he!'

The blue eye twinkled. 'I am generally fortunate, I believe, but there is always a risk.'

'Did you purchase Herringham with your winnings?' Kit demanded, his blazing brown eyes meeting that cool blue one.

Ignoring the impertinent nature of the question the Major said calmly: 'I was fortunate enough to have had a recent run of luck, certainly.'

'At my brother's expense?'

'Among others,' replied the Major, unperturbed.

'Among others!' echoed the young man, flushing darkly. 'And how many others have you ruined?'

'As far as I know, none,' responded the other gently. 'Your brother was in debt to persons throughout the town.'

'But you did not hesitate to purchase his estate,' persisted Kit, unable now to curb the flow.

'I gave him an excellent price,' the Major said, his eye fixed on the young man's face. 'In fact, you should be grateful to me for having taken such a burden off your hands!'

'How . . . how *dare* you!' stammered Kit, scarlet with suppressed violence. 'You do not know how I struggled to maintain the place!'

'I can guess,' responded Andrew, refusing to be drawn. 'And if you made such efforts you should know full well what I have taken on. You need not concern yourself that I mean to let the estate fall to ruin. I have every intention of making it solvent, and I had hoped I might rely on your help.'

'Go to the devil!' cried Kit, reaching the door just as it opened. Almost colliding with the startled Keen he brought himself up short, muttered something unintelligible, and left.

'Kit!' exclaimed Alicia, gaining the hall as her brother burst from the library. 'What is it? What has happened?'

He stopped and regarded her fulminatingly. 'Your friend,' he answered harshly. 'Come outside, I want to talk to you.'

She allowed herself to be propelled from the house, but descending the steps she pulled her arm from his grasp. 'You're hurting me,' she protested, drawing back from him. 'What is this about?'

He turned to face her, at once contrite. 'Forgive me! It was thoughtless. Only do come, before I go mad!'

'Very well, but I wish you would calm yourself, dearest. It cannot be good for you to get so excited.'

He laughed bitterly. 'Just like Mama, dear Ally! Never mind, I forgive you. Come on!' He took her arm again, but gently, and hurried her down the steps and across the long grass. She made an attempt to hold her skirt out of the wet and failed. Realising her brother was not his usual self she said nothing, permitting him to hurry her towards an outcrop of trees beyond the south lawn. Within their shelter he stopped, and Alicia, reflecting that her skirt was ruined anyway, leant against the trunk of a tree and panted.

'Now,' she said, when her breathing became easier, 'what is this about?'

'Your friend,' replied her brother harshly, 'your Major! He's no gentleman, Ally, that's certain! He's a damned Captain Sharp, told me so himself!'

'A card-cheat?' exclaimed Alicia, paling a little. 'Oh, come, Kit, surely not! Surely he did not tell you so himself!' As she spoke she realised, with a sinking feeling, that it would be quite like the Major to say such a thing of himself.

But Kit's reply was: 'Not exactly, I admit, but he did say he purchased Herringham with his winnings! And had the gall to imply it was a bad bargain! I tell you, Ally, I felt inclined to have his blood for it!'

'Really, Kit!' exclaimed Alicia in half-laughing alarm. 'You should not say such things, even in jest!'

He relaxed a little. 'No, I should not. I know it myself, but I tell you, Ally, the fellow makes my blood boil! What do you know of him, besides what he tells you?'

'Nothing,' she admitted, 'but—'

'But nothing!' interrupted her brother remorselessly.

'The fellow could be a deserter for all we know! Why, there is no proof that he is even who he says he is!'

'There is the paper,' faltered Alicia. 'And as for his being Major Harbury, well, couldn't we find out some-how? Ask someone?'

'Who?' he demanded derisively. 'You don't know the first thing about the fellow.'

'I believe his father is a peer,' she replied defensively.

Kit frowned. 'Did the fellow tell you that?'

She flushed slightly. 'No, as a matter of fact he didn't. Papa knew a Lord Harbury, though. I'm sure of it.'

The flush was not lost on Kit. 'Denied it, did he? Well, at least that's honest.'

'He didn't, actually,' said Alicia, who could recall with startling clarity the whole of her conversation with the gentleman. 'As a matter of fact he has only ever told me two definite things about himself.'

'And what were they?' enquired her brother, his lip curling mockingly.

She met his gaze squarely. 'He said first that he was an agent,' she answered simply. She was startled to see his colour change rapidly as he searched her face.

'An agent?' he echoed faintly. And then, more strong-ly: 'For whom? Did he tell you that, too?'

She smiled. 'No, though for some reason he would have me believe him a traitor.'

To her surprise he laughed. 'But you don't, I collect! Ally, what hold has this fellow over you? You were never wont to be so easily taken-in!'

She considered him for a moment. 'He is kind,' she said at last, 'and very fair to us. It is not his fault our affairs are in such a mess.'

'Perhaps not, but he has not helped!'

She smiled gently at him. 'Dearest, why are you behaving like this? Don't you know we could never have kept Herringham? You tried, I know you did, but there was nothing anyone could do! You shouldn't reproach yourself.'

He laughed again. 'You don't know, Ally! My God, if only I had been a little sooner! I could have saved it!'

The alarm returned. 'Kit, what are you talking of?'

His eyes flickered to her face and away again. 'I . . . I had an idea that might have worked,' he said at last. 'Don't ask me, Ally, for I shall not tell you. If only . . .' He frowned, and then turned to her. 'Ally, the fellow likes you. Could you not persuade him to let us buy back the estate?'

She laughed unsteadily. 'Kit, are you run mad? How could we ever do such a thing, even assuming he would wish to sell?'

'There is a way,' he answered vaguely. 'Could you do it?'

'No,' she said firmly, moving away from the tree. 'Kit, I do not know what you are planning, but everything you say worries me further! I pray it is not something illegal!'

He turned on her angrily. 'Do you think so well of me, then, that you prefer to trust this . . . this adventurer before your own brother?'

'Of course not, Kit! But you are not being sensible! Can you not see that we are better out of it?'

'No, I cannot! And you surprise me, Ally, truly you do! I had not thought you could turn so easily from your own!'

Angered at last she turned to face him. 'I have not "turned from my own", Kit, and if you had more sense you would see it is not so.' For a moment she regarded him coldly, and then she turned, and lifting her skirt once more she crossed the lawn towards the house, her train trailing in the wet grass.

# CHAPTER
# FOUR

NEARING Court had come into the possession of the Harbury family only recently. Guy, father to the present owner, had taken the lease when a sudden piece of great fortune at piquet had put an abrupt end to all his financial worries. Compared with other country estates, Nearing was not large, but it was possessed of a certain charm in its compact Georgian elegance, and when the opportunity had presented itself for Lord Harbury to purchase he had hesitated no longer than to discover that to do so would not send his family to Queer Street once more.

Here the two Harbury boys, Paul and Andrew, had been born, and here they had passed their early years, and, later, the long vacation. To them it represented all that was secure about their family. Here had Guy Harbury died, peacefully, of a sudden chill. His widow, Miranda, had at once fallen into protracted grief from which the presence of her eldest son and his wife could not draw her. For several months she had not ventured from its walls, ignoring all the requests of her family to do so. At last, however, she seemed a little to recover from her loss. Corinna, the new Lady Harbury, was expecting her first child, and of course, Mama would now be needed. During the months that followed Corinna had several times to repress the impatience she felt with the older woman. She had always had a horror of being cossetted, and the fact that she felt really better now than ever before made dear Mama's solicitude sometimes hard to bear. When nothing suited Corinna more than a brisk walk in the Park Mama would beg her to lie down; and when all she desired was a substantial meal Mama would encourage her to seek her bed with a bowl of thin gruel. She bore it patiently, however, and such was her husband's relief that his mother had at last found something to occupy her that she forbore to tell him just how often she felt like screaming her frustrations to the four winds.

The marriage was a happy one. Corinna was ever high-spirited and Paul, a doting husband, content to indulge her. They had enjoyed several successful seasons in the Metropolis, although it had seemed at first as though an early indiscretion would have banished them forever. They had been discovered in the vestibule at Almack's in a passionate embrace, by no less a personage than the Princess Esterhazy, wife of the Austrian Ambassador, and for a while there had been some concern that they would not again be admitted. Although Corinna had stated quite unequivocally that the idea of being a social outcast vastly appealed to her she had been secretly concerned, and it had been a relief to all when some private communications from Miranda had smoothed the path.

The imminent arrival of a young Harbury had prevented their presence in London this year and consequently, when news of a disturbing nature reached Caroline, or Caro as she was commonly called, the daughter of Guy Harbury's sister, she had instantly pulled forth pen and paper to write a note to her dearest Paul. At first the young peer had been puzzled to have such an epistle addressed to him. Caro's letters were always long, and often involved, being largely concerned with the progress of her various offspring. What she could possibly have to say that would be of interest to a mere male he could not conjecture, and had his wife been within call he would have instantly handed the missive to her. She was not, however, and so, stifling a sigh, he had borne the letter to his study, there to peruse it at his leisure. As he had expected the communication took some deciphering, but when he had dismissed his cousin's demands for news the second paragraph caused him sharply to draw in his breath and read the small, close writing with greater attention. The news she conveyed was disturbing and the young peer was momentarily undecided on his course of action. So great was his abstraction that he did not instantly hear the click of the door, and his wife was beside him before he knew she was in the room.

'That looks like Caro's writing,' she remarked, bending with a little difficulty to kiss his cheek. Her time was not far distant.

Her husband looked up and smiled. 'So it is! And it's taken me this half-hour to fathom! But I thought you were resting, love.'

Corinna shook her head and smiled. 'Mama is lying down, and I am relying on you not to betray me! What does Caro say that is so engrossing?'

His smile faded and he shook his head. 'It may be something or quite nothing. I can't tell. Listen. "I have heard some news about dear Andy that I do not understand. Some gossip has reached my Charlie about a certain Gareth Kenyon. The name means nought to me, but I daresay it might to you as you and Andy are brothers."'

'That is typical of Caro's reasoning,' remarked Corinna with a smile.

'Shush, love. "For some reason he is worried about Andy's involvement in the wretched fellow's demise, though how that is I cannot surmise, since it seems the unfortunate man died in some kind of drunken brawl. The hub of the matter is that Andy had some involvement with the said Kenyon, that is, he gave him money for some property in Sussex. There was some doubt about how he came by the money, though if I know Andy it was in some card game! But the aforementioned Kenyon was indignant after the event about how Andy had acquired the property. Charlie is concerned that Andy has apparently disappeared, being last seen when he was, quite unaccountably it seems to me, summoned to Horseguards. Constables came to us one morning asking for Andy, but although they said they would return they have not yet done so, for which I am heartily thankful, since one of them was a most disagreeable man, implying in the most odious fashion that I was lying, and had concealed our Andy in some attic or other! As if he would consent to such treatment! But where he is no one knows. Now, dear Paul, do not panic, but Charlie suggests you might discover something about our dear Andrew, perhaps from one of your Government friends? I don't know about these things, but Charlie says you would know what to do."' Paul sighed and laid aside the paper. 'She talks a great deal about the children, but you may read that at your leisure.'

A frown puckered Corinna's brow. 'Paul, I don't understand!'

He gathered her to him and she put an arm around his shoulder as he sat. 'No more do I, but I must go to London.' He looked up anxiously. 'Darling, can you forgive me? I shall be back in two or three days, I promise, long before you need me.'

She smiled and ruffled his blond hair. 'How many times, my love, must I tell you that I am really perfectly well! In fact, I have seldom felt so fit, and you know I hate being fussed! Besides, if you did not go you would be quite unbearable!'

He rose and kissed her, thinking as he did so how lovely she looked. She was lucky. Her pregnancy had been easy. 'Do you mind very much? I thought when he entered the Army my troubles would be over! However, I cannot let this be.' He flicked the sheet carelessly and sighed. 'Do not tell mother. You know how she cares for Andy. He really is so like Papa!'

'And she has never ceased to miss him.'

'No. I think Caro's idea about the card game is probably right. He has all father's skill, and more, and you know how father got this house!'

She smiled up at him affectionately. 'Dear Mama never tires of telling me!' She frowned. 'Paul, you must go to London! Wherever can he be?'

He shook his head. 'I cannot conceive. It is not like him. How unfortunate that the wretched fellow had to die!'

Corinna frowned. 'Do you remember him, love? I cannot say that I do!'

'No. Was Andy there when he died, I wonder!'

The brown eyes widened. 'Paul, you are not suggesting Andy was involved?'

He smiled and flicked her cheek. 'No, love, of course not! I am convinced his death had nothing to do with it. What an unfortunate affair! But I shall find out where he is, never fear. Now, will you go to your couch? Or must I summon mother?'

'No, do not! You know how she fusses me! Very well, I shall go, but only if you will come up with me! After all, I am to lose you tomorrow!' She looked up at him, the beautiful brown eyes anxious. 'You will find him, won't you, dearest? It would break mother's heart if anything happened to him.'

'I know,' he answered grimly. 'If there's anything to

discover I shall, don't worry! And now, are you going to rest?'

She smiled, and put her arm around his waist. Together they left the room.

# CHAPTER
# FIVE

AN uneasy peace reigned at Herringham. When the
three members of the party met at meal-times Kit's
obvious determination to converse with neither his sister
nor his host made things no easier. One evening he
excused himself sullenly before the port was served.
Neither the Major nor Alicia remarked on, or appeared
to notice the impulse that caused him to remove an
orange from the dish on the dining table, and a small
untouched leg of lamb from one of the side tables. Alicia
kept her eyes bent on her plate and Andrew impercept-
ibly summoned Keen to replenish their glasses. There
was a definite lessening of tension as the door closed
behind the young man. It seemed an interminable time
before Keen had served his master to his satisfaction,
setting the port and glass within his reach and finally
withdrawing when the Major said: 'Thank you, Keen,
I'll ring when I need you.' Turning to Alicia he remarked
conversationally: 'I take it your brother is at outs with
the both of us.'

She sighed, and began twisting the slim stem of her
wine glass. 'I can't understand him! He was always so
sensible, so . . . so mature for his age! Now—! Well, he
seems so like Gary I can hardly recognise him!' She
regarded him frankly. 'I'm sure he has some wild scheme
in mind! If only it may not land him in serious trouble!'

The Major regarded her gravely. 'He has given you no
idea of what it could be?'

She shook her head. 'No, but he talks all the time of saving Herringham, so it must be something serious, mustn't it, otherwise how could he even contemplate such a thing?'

The Major could not reply, and, exchanging wine for port proceeded to turn over the problem in his mind.

He had always known the young man would be troublesome. He had undertaken the mission fully aware that he would in all likelihood be confronting idealism in its strongest form, but he had been unprepared for the fever of anxiety that had the young man quite in its grip. Before the appearance in his life of Miss Alicia Kenyon he would not have scrupled to send such a foolish young man to the rightabout, but of late his course of action, at once so plain, had become unobligingly clouded. He did not have to search very far to discover the reason for this indecision, and beguiled several minutes as he lay in bed that night thinking of her as she had looked with the candle-light caressing her features. He had always had an eye for a pretty face—in fact, it had been his entanglement with one such that had precipitated his entry into the Army—but his former light o' loves had always been of quite a different class. Ladies of Quality he had always avoided. They posed too many problems for a single gentleman like himself, and tended to regard any light-hearted flirtation most seriously. At first Andrew had believed himself to have been seized by some fancy that would pass in a few days, and had then decided that he must completely have lost his reason. It had taken him really a very short time to realise, however, that his present affliction was none of these things, that he was indulging in no light-hearted flirtation, in fact in no flirtation at all. Of course she complicated matters. What chance would he have with the sister if his evidence helped to send the brother to the scaffold? For such it would, he had no doubt. He was quite well aware that the young man had no sympathies with the Bonaparte cause, that his traitorous activities had arisen purely from a hopeless desire to save his home. He saw in them the last despairing attempts of a boy to achieve what must always have been impossible, and knew that it behoved him to rescue the young man, if possible with no stain on his character. And all this while the young man was so actively hostile against him! With his co-operation it would have been easy. The name of his connection in London, the trap prepared and baited. But always there was Alicia, Alicia in the middle, who, despite her suspicions, could not be told the truth. Oh, but it was too troublesome! The letter would arrive, and some response would result. Until then, therefore, he must bide his time.

The morning brought a diversion. Alicia, being awakened as usual by the sound of Sally drawing the curtains, was surprised to observe that maiden struggling vainly in an attempt to suppress tears. All attempts ceased upon her mistress inquiring, in a voice of concern, whether anything were amiss. The tears spilled over and Sally, keeping her face averted, silently shook her head. Convinced now that something was seriously wrong Alicia threw back the bedclothes and swung her feet to the ground. 'Sally!' she said firmly, causing the girl to jerk up her head. 'Tell me what is the matter? Has something upset you?'

Again the girl shook her head. 'No, ma'am, 'tis nothing. Will you have your chocolate?'

A tray reposed on the nearby table, but Alicia ignored both this and the maid's reference to it. 'How can I help you, Sally if you won't tell me what's the matter?' she asked gently.

At last the girl met that clear gaze. 'It's Mrs Carter,

ma'am,' she said simply. 'Some things are missing from the larder, meat, 'n cheese, 'n bread, too, and then there's Mr Kenyon's bedclothes!'

'Mr Kenyon's *bedclothes*?' echoed Alicia, startled.

The girl nodded. 'Extra ones he had, asked for them specially. An' now they're gone, ma'am! What with me doing Mr Kenyon's room yesterday Mrs Carter came to thinking I must've taken them, an' the food, too!'

Alicia said nothing, and her protracted silence served to convince the girl that Miss Kenyon likewise was confident of her guilt. She hung her head again and Alicia, who had in fact been thinking deeply, was startled by the sound of smothered sobs. 'Don't cry,' she said briskly, standing up. 'I know it wasn't you, and I shall tell Mrs Carter as much as soon as I am dressed.' She grasped the mug of chocolate, dutifully sipped at it, and then turned again to the girl. 'Could you help me, please? I will wear my grey cambric.'

Some minutes later Miss Kenyon, properly arrayed, her hair dressed in a simple knot on the top of her head, proceeded in the direction of the kitchens. She had no compunction about taking matters into her own hands, even though she was, in fact, no longer mistress but merely a guest, since she suspected the affair nearly concerned her brother. Properly, she should first have consulted with the Major, but her reason yet told her to beware of trusting too completely one so little known, whatever her instincts might tell her.

She found Mrs Carter in the kitchens, drawing fresh-baked and steaming bread from the large, old-fashioned oven. She waited while the woman set the loaves to cool, her nostrils savouring the delicious smell that pervaded these lower regions. At first the housekeeper failed to notice the presence of her former mistress, so occupied was she, but presently she saw her from the corner of her eye and, leaving what she had been doing she came forward at once, wiping her hands on an already grubby apron.

'Beg pardon, Miss Alicia, I dint straightways see you there. What can I do to be of help?'

Alicia smiled. 'That's all right, Mrs Carter, I know how busy you must be.'

'Ay, so I am! There's mention of a fancy chef coming from Lunnon-way, kitchen-maids, too, though I'll believe that when I see 'em! Proper glad I s'll be when I can get back to my own work, what with that Sally takin' Mr Christopher's bedclothes, an' all! No shame, these modern girls, an' I thought her a right 'un, an' all! However, you never can tell. Windmills in her head, she's got.'

'That's what I came to talk to you about, Mrs Carter,' said Alicia, stepping boldly in as the housekeeper paused to take breath. 'Sally told me what had happened, and I must tell you that I think her innocent of taking the bedclothes and the food.'

'Well!' exclaimed Mrs Carter, flushing darkly. 'An' if the little minx aint been telling tales! Can't trust 'em at all, these local girls!'

'She wouldn't have told me at all, Mrs Carter, you know, had I not asked her about it. She was very upset.'

'Humph! She had every reason to be.'

'I do think you have been a little hasty, however,' said Alicia quickly before Mrs Carter could start again. 'I believe she had nothing to do with the disappearances. In fact, I believe someone quite different to have been responsible.'

Mrs Carter's colour increased. 'An' who might that be?' she demanded, eyeing her mistress with every appearance of preparing to do battle.

'My brother,' replied Alicia coolly, refusing to be intimidated.

Mrs Carter was instantly taken aback. '*Master Christopher*?' she said faintly. 'Nay, Miss Alicia, why should he want to do such a thing?'

Since Miss Kenyon had not the smallest notion she decided to take a high-handed attitude, saying loftily: 'That need not concern you, Mrs Carter. Suffice it to say that the girl Sally is innocent. I hope the matter may now be considered closed.'

Repressing her indignation at the sudden change of front Mrs Carter bobbed, and said nothing. Thinking that she had said enough Alicia nodded at the woman to continue her baking and, turning, left the kitchen.

Greatly perplexed by what she had heard Alicia walked slowly back up the stairs. She truly believed her brother to have been responsible—his behaviour since his return had been odd enough for her to believe even stranger things of him—but she was quite unable to account for this latest development. She had herself seen him remove a leg of lamb from a side-table last evening, and although considering such a thing strange she had merely assumed her brother to be still hungry, yet unwilling to share the table with them any longer. Gaining the ground floor at last she determined to go in search of him. It was yet early, barely nine o'clock, so she was confident of finding him still in his chamber, in fact, barely awake. This seemed to be the case when no answer came to her repeated knockings, so she opened the door a little and peered in. Contrary to her expectation the room was flooded with light, and she had a clear view of the entire room. Her brother was not there. Entering quickly now she crossed to the adjoining dressing room and, after knocking perfunctorily, satisfied herself that he was not there either. Frowning, she turned back slowly into the room and contemplated the unruffled bed. She could not help believing that her brother had not slept there that night.

Seriously alarmed, she ran without thinking to the room she knew to be occupied by Major Harbury and knocked urgently upon the door until she heard some movement within. The Major proved to be fully dressed, a fact Miss Kenyon did not reflect upon, merely pouring out her story that Kit was not in his room as soon as he opened the door. Andrew frowned fleetingly, and then, his features relaxed again, stepped calmly into the passage and closed the door.

'Can you be sure?' he inquired, taking her arm and leading her gently towards the stairs. 'Perhaps he has risen early and gone for a walk. Or a ride, perhaps.'

'But his bed is made!' Alicia protested, annoyed that he should be so little concerned.

He smiled now. 'Is that so very extraordinary? You do not know, perhaps he may even have made it himself as an effort towards economy. I have heard of more unusual things, I must admit.'

While doubting whether he would know how Alicia was forced to admit that it was possible, acknowledging to herself that her brother had been behaving so strangely of late that almost anything was possible. The Major's cool manner was beginning to calm her now. She saw that she had indeed been precipitate, foolish even, in concluding that because he was not then in his chamber he had not been there at all. 'You are right, of course,' she said, forcing herself to speak calmly. 'How silly you must think me! I cannot imagine how I came to think such a thing!'

'You are overwrought,' he responded at once, 'and greatly concerned about your brother. It is quite natural. However, I do not believe you have anything to worry about just now.' He smiled at her as they descended. 'Have you breakfasted?' he inquired politely. 'No?

Neither have I. I suggest we do so without delay. These matters are too weighty to discuss whilst hungry.'

Submitting, Alicia followed him to the breakfast room and permitted her anxieties to die away as she consumed a light meal.

Before long, however, her doubts returned, and she mounted the stairs to fetch her wrap. There was no reason why he should not go for a walk, or a ride, she would just feel easier if she could be certain. And then what should happen but that she should meet him, just as she rounded the house towards the shrubbery. He was striding confidently towards her from the direction of the old labourer's cottage, the cottage that had been demolished, where Gary and Kit had played when they were boys and from whence she had always been banished because she was a girl. She had watched them, through, from the safety of the shrubbery. For several years after the roof had given way the walls had stood, stark and proud, and she had seen her brothers playing at soldiers on these battlements. Their cousin Gregory had been willingly admitted to these adventures. He had been older than Kit, younger than Gary, but possessed of a natural leadership that had won admiration, albeit grudging and reluctant, from the older boy. To Kit he had been a hero. Kit's broken shoulder had put a stop to the marauding hordes for ever, for Papa declared the site to be dangerous, and the walls had been torn down. The boys had still gone there, although only a few random stones remained, but Alicia had started to grow up and had lost interest in spying on her brothers. Besides, they would be gone for hours. She had wondered vaguely how they had managed to pass the time, but her interest had waned with the years.

He saw her now, and she thought for a moment that he hesitated. Then he came forward again, a frown on his

face. She was conscious of his top boots, and that he bore
something in his hand. Now he came to her, his expression defiant.

'What's the matter, Ally? Spying on me again?'

She flushed slightly, and tried to smile. 'Of course not!
Though I did wonder where you were.'

'Walking,' he answered shortly.

She nodded. 'I thought so. Dearest, there has been an
upset at the house. Some food has disappeared. Was it
you?'

Suspiciously he eyed her. 'What's this, Ally? The
Inquisition?'

She essayed a laugh. 'Don't be nonsensical! No doubt
you were hungry, but you should tell Mrs Carter, you
know, if you go to her larder, for she has to plan ahead,
and it is hard enough for her anyway.'

'Well, I was hungry,' he replied, seemingly with reluctance.

'But that's not all, Kit. Apparently some bedclothes
are missing also! Sally was very upset. It seems Mrs
Carter accused her of taking them, but she swears she
did not.'

'Alicia, what is this?' Kit Kenyon demanded, his
temper rapidly fraying. 'Why are you interrogating me?
How can I possibly be responsible for bed-covers?'

'I don't know, dear,' his sister responded patiently,
'but it seems you asked for them particularly, which is
why Mrs Carter noticed they were gone.'

'What, is the world run mad? Tell the woman to sort
out her own problems! Leave me be, Alicia!' So saying
he pushed past her on his way to the house, leaving her
to puzzle over his extraordinary behaviour. It was not
until he had been gone several minutes that she realised
he had been carrying an empty decanter.

Puzzled and perplexed Alicia moved into the shrubbery walk, and sat down upon the hard wooden bench set there many years before. The shrubbery was extensive, and Alicia's view was of many bushes of varying heights all now sadly in need of care and attention. Without the restraining hand of an experienced gardener the little bushes had grown tightly together, sending out wild, untamed branches in all directions, so that a solid wall now faced her. Her mind full, she sat unseeing on her hard seat. How easy it would be, she thought, to let it all flow over her, to care for nought, to let her life pass by without noticing. It was so still in the shrubbery! She did not notice the chill in the air, nor the gentle breeze that stirred the branches around her and pulled free one strand of hair to flutter against her cheek. Her eyes closed, her mind almost totally blank, she sat motionless upon her hard seat, until it was borne in upon her that she was shivering with cold. Her wrap had slipped unnoticed from her shoulders and now lay in a pile of dead leaves behind the bench. Stooping, she caught it up and drew it tightly about her shoulders. Then she made her way briskly from the shrubbery.

Approaching the house she was somewhat surprised to see a coach, laden with a number of valises and bags, approaching very steadily up the untidy avenue. For a moment she thought, hoped, that it might be Avery, and then realised that no lawyer would arrive so heavily encumbered with baggage. The vehicle had by this time gained the front of the house and Alicia, feeling in some sense mistress still, hastened to greet the guest.

It was her cousin. As she approached the carriage she heard his voice from the interior, and in a moment the dapper individual known as his valet had descended, and was turning to help his master, Beau Kenyon, tall and elegant, a lace handkerchief pressed delicately to his lips. With an air of exquisite boredom he surveyed the house before him, and, pocketing the handkerchief with due care, turned in a leisurely manner to greet his cousin.

'Alicia, my sweet! What is this I hear?'

Coolly Alicia regarded him. He had never been a favourite with her and she said somewhat tartly: 'What is all what, Gregory?'

He looked pained. 'My sweet, your letter! The news that our dearest Gareth has left us! Indeed, I was from town, or I should have been here the sooner.'

Invariably he irritated her, and now she said with an effort at civility: 'No, how silly of me! It is good of you to come, Gregory, but perhaps you did not fully understand? Herringham is no longer ours, you know.'

The Beau sighed. 'Alas! Then it is true? I had hoped for some error, some mistake to be discovered, but evidently it is not to be.' He swallowed, and closed his eyes for a moment. 'Alicia, dear coz, delightful though this is, might I be permitted to enter? The chaise, you know, the interminable swaying.'

'Of course!' Alicia exclaimed, her eyes dancing. 'How thoughtless I am! I own, Gregory, it is so long since we met that I had forgot your hatred of travelling. Have you come far?'

He shook his head, and instantly grimaced. 'From the village, my sweet, is all, but far enough. I stayed overnight at some abominable hostelry. The food! And then these Sussex roads of yours!' Clasping his cane more tightly he followed her up the steps and into the hall. He raised one brow at the sight of the emptiness that greeted him. In another instant they were met by Keen, who, having heard the sounds of an arrival, had hurried from below to be of service. For a moment Beau Kenyon regarded him with dislike and deep suspicion, and then appeared to recognise him, favouring him with a nod.

'Keen,' he enunciated, holding out gloves and cane. 'You may take my coat.'

Approval thus signified, the ageing butler hurried forward to remove the many-caped great-coat that had swathed its owner from chin to heel. Watching anxiously as the man bore away the treasured garment, he failed to notice the library door open and that a figure stood there framed.

Major Harbury had leisure to observe his guest. He was tall, nearly six feet, and turned out in the height of elegance. From the intricacies of a snowy cravat to the dove-grey pantaloons and gleaming Hessians all was perfection, and as he now handed his hat with great care to his manservant the Major was able to observe the order to which the glowing chestnut locks had been arranged. Then the face was turned, and the Major caught a glimpse of sharp brown eyes before the languid lids were lowered. He was a not ill-looking man of six-and-twenty, with a strong, high-cheekboned face and slightly curved nose. His complexion was at that moment pale. Observing his host he stepped forward with surprising fluidity of movement and extended one long and well-manicured hand.

'Harbury, I believe. No, Alicia, you do not need to introduce us, we are acquainted.'

The Major bowed.

'I trust I am not inconveniencing you unduly,' pronounced the Beau, evidently feeling some explanation to be necessary, 'but I am come in answer to such a letter, my dear Major, from my delightful cousin. What she spoke of intrigued me so greatly I could not resist!' He turned to smile at his cousin and at that moment caught sight of a figure at the head of the stairs.

'Greg!' exclaimed Kit, hurrying down. 'Thank heaven you are come!'

# CHAPTER
# SIX

RAISING the quizzing glass that hung on a black riband around his neck the Beau surveyed the rapidly descending figure.

'Christopher,' he pronounced as the young man gained the hall. 'You seem almost pleased to see me.'

Kit flushed but said: 'Indeed I am! That is, I mean . . . Oh, dash it all, Gregory, I can't explain now!'

'Pray do not,' replied the other, suppressing a yawn. 'I have been so besieged by tales of distress, my Christopher, that I have dragged myself out at some unearthly hour to come to your sister's aid! And now I find it is all in vain. No,' he raised a hand, for Kit had opened his mouth to protest, 'all explanations must wait. If the dear Major will excuse me I shall retire to my chamber. A few hours rest will admirably refresh me.'

He moved towards the stairs on the words but Christopher laid a hand on his arm. 'I say, Greg, damn it all—'

'Christopher,' pronounced the Beau in pained accents, 'you rumple my sleeve.'

Exasperated, Kit removed his hand from the coat of blue superfine and turned from his cousin with a gesture of annoyance.

For a second a frown flickered across that pale countenance, and then Gregory Kenyon said: 'After breakfast, my dear, tomorrow. You may talk as much as you wish. But now—!' Dramatically he raised one hand to his brow and proceeded to mount the stairs, his valet before him.

'He will be disappointed,' Alicia remarked, with a little laugh. 'His room cannot be prepared.'

'It is,' Kit replied unexpectedly. 'I asked Sally to do it yesterday.'

'Kit!' exclaimed his sister, staring at him. 'How could you possibly know?'

'Instinct, I suppose,' he said, and walked away.

For Kit the day proved interminable. Wherever he went his sister or the Major would be discovered, waiting to pounce on him, to question him, and when in desperation he went into the Park he knew that the Major's man had followed him, was spying on him, as usual.

It had been a shock to discover the little man's existence. At first Kit had thought it a coincidence that wherever he was the little batman was also, and then, hearing a soft rustle behind him in the grass one day he had known he was being followed. He employed cunning to throw off his pursuer, and this generally proved successful. It was lucky that they seemed not yet to have discovered the secret stairway from the house, but it was always a risk that one or other of them would chance on him as he left the house by the hidden door.

Once when he was going to Gerande the little man had come upon him in the shrubbery, and he had had to walk over the trap door and on, praying that the metal ring would not be seen. It was not, the little man had followed him, but it had been an anxious moment, and he had had to take more care. Just now it did not matter. He had been to Gerande already, would not be going again until evening.

Despondently he surveyed the house from a little promontory. It was a dismal sight. From here he could clearly see that the roof needed repair, that the east wing, unused for several years, would take a deal of money to put to rights, more money than he could hope to find, even if Herringham were once again his. For a moment he wondered if he had been mad even to consider saving it. From here the task seemed phenomenal, beyond him. And the risks he had run, all for stone, for his sister, who did not even care! Sinking where he stood, he buried his head in his hands as the enormity of what he had done struck him. He could feel the eyes of the little batman boring into his skull, but was unable to care. Gradually, however, the despair evaporated, the optimism that had buoyed him all those weeks returning at last to help him. Gregory had come, Gregory who was so fearless, so clever, as brave and cunning as Gerande himself, who would deal so simply with the threat of the Major, leaving the way clear for himself, and safety for Alicia. Gregory, who had involved him with promises of great wealth, of recognition when the invading forces arrived, of gratitude from the Emperor himself.

Suddenly he felt sickened. What was he about, betraying his own, and for such a cause? Why, he did not even believe in it! Atrocities, murder, bloodshed, the stuff of revolution revolted him. With an effort he thought of Herringham, of saving it, of succeeding where Gary, whom he had despised, had failed. It was a lucky recollection. Standing up he surveyed the noble edifice once more, seeing it as it must once have been, how it would be again when it was his. Stronger now he walked down the little hill towards the house, refusing to glance in the direction of the little valet's hunched figure.

Alicia descended to dinner in some perplexity. She had tried vainly for some little time to discover a reason for her cousin's sudden appearance at Herringham. Knowing him as she did she could not for a moment accept that he would suffer the tortuous journey from

London in a fit of cousinly concern. Neither had her brother's extraordinary behaviour on his arrival gone unnoticed. It was perfectly clear that he had been expecting him, and that he regarded his arrival as the answer to whatever it was that troubled him. Alicia's unease grew. She disliked the Beau, but had never, until now, realised how possessed he was of native cunning. She had known him to be clever, and had, as a child, suffered much from his mocking tongue, but had never until this moment suspected anything but mockery in him. Perhaps it was the situation, the fact that she was so worried about her brother, that made her sense danger in every little thing, but she could not but regard her cousin's arrival with foreboding. If only Gareth, unreliable, careless Gareth, had been alive at least he would have been somewhere to turn. But Gareth, as usual, was not there when he was needed. Gareth had chosen this moment to die, falling in a drunken stupor from the balcony of his own rooms.

Gaining the drawing room she found that her cousin had not yet descended, but that her brother and the Major were present, and not conversing. The Major had taken up a position near to the fire, one arm lying along the mantel shelf. Kit was seated at some distance from him, but there was disappointment on his face when he saw his sister, and he laid aside his book and stood up with apparent reluctance.

'Have you seen Greg?' he demanded, coming to her with some impatience.

She smiled perfunctorily and said: 'I fear he will be late, Major. He generally takes so very long over his toilet that he almost invariably keeps us waiting.'

But the door opened as she spoke and admitted the Beau, complete to a shade in biscuit-coloured pantaloons, with a nice selection of fobs and seals at his

waistband, and a cravat of intricate, although not os-
tentatious, design. He raised his quizzing glass as he
stood on the threshold, scanned the assembled company, and sighed. Letting fall the glass he stepped into
the chamber, an expression of boredom belied by the
gleam of dark eyes beneath the carefully lazy lids.

'Greg! What an age you have been!'

Turning towards his young cousin the Beau raised his
quizzing glass again, levelled it at Kit, and let it fall. 'I
warned you, my dear Christopher, that I should not be
seen. My constitution, as you must be aware, is not
suited to your Sussex roads.'

'Well, I know, but dash it all, Greg—' He stopped,
quelled by a dagger glance from beneath those deceptive
lids. The Major watched, fascinated. 'I suppose you are
right,' Kit said sullenly, turning his back.

'Indeed, coz, I almost invariably am.' With a graceful
movement the Beau turned from the boy to bow over
Alicia's hand. 'Dearest Alicia, radiant as ever! How wise
of you to have put off your weeds! Black does not suit
you, and it is, I daresay, an outmoded custom.'

The malice was evident, and Alicia felt sufficiently
goaded to say: 'You, I notice, do not wear arm-bands! I,
at least, am in half-mourning!'

He smiled at her. 'True, my dearest coz! You are
right, as always! But Gareth! Ah, my dear cousin, we
were never close! Tis true, I regret his passing, but how
long, do you suppose, would he have regretted mine? I
concern myself more with those he has left.' He smiled a
peculiarly cold smile, and the Major noticed that the
watchfulness had yet to leave his eyes, that their expression, although indeed brimful of mockery and derision,
was yet wary, and uncertain.

The Major conducted Alicia into the dining room,
seating her at the foot of the table, with the Beau and Kit

on either side of him. It was not a particularly cosy gathering, he thought, surveying first Kit's sullen countenance, and then the Beau's guarded one.

Throughout the meal Alicia was conscious of the tension between them. Only the Major seemed entirely at his ease, and she remembered that it had been his casual manner that she had observed first in him. He seemed wholly unaffected by Kit's sulky silence or by the Beau's occasional, malice-loaded comments. Had she not been persuaded that he was always on the alert she might have supposed him to be half asleep. She glanced at her cousin, meeting a dark, glittering look that made her wonder. She raised her chin a little.

'Faith, cousin,' the Beau said, shaking his head, 'I believe you grow more fine with every year! Would that Gareth had left you a fortune!'

She raised one brow at him. 'Why, Gregory? Would you have made me an offer?'

'Of course!' he answered her at once, some of the derision fading from his eyes as he smiled. 'I always had half a mind to you, cousin! I do not believe society has seen your equal.'

'Fine speaking, Gregory, but it won't fadge! I doubt if you will ever marry, unless, of course, she is possessed of some fifty-thousand a year!'

He laughed. 'The trouble of it is, Alicia, that heiresses are invariably possessed of a squint, or some other deformity!'

Alicia started to laugh, glancing without thought at the Major's shadowed countenance, and the laugh stifled in her throat. She blushed and bent her head over her plate.

The Beau gave a low chuckle, glanced sideways at his host, who remained impassive, and returned his attention to the meal.

Alicia, after dinner, retired to her mother's sitting room where she had assembled those household accounts Mrs Carter had passed on to her for settlement. It was here that her cousin, some while later, discovered her, knocking gently and entering without waiting for a reply. Alicia, on the floor surrounded by papers, sat back on her heels with a frown of annoyance on her face. She disliked Gregory, and resented his interruption when she still had much to do. If he noticed her expression he gave no sign of it, merely smiling at her, and saying: 'A charming picture, indeed! Do not move, pray, on my account!'

She had risen now, and impatiently shook out her skirts.

'What do you want, Gregory? If it is merely to talk I must tell you that I am exceedingly busy, and have a great deal to do if I am to leave our affairs in any order for the Major!'

His eyes glinted at her, and a mocking smile lifted one side of his thin mouth. 'For the Major! I wonder, my dear Alicia, that you are so concerned. You cannot love him overmuch.'

She shrugged. 'Perhaps not, but it is not his fault, after all, and if he truly does intend to put Herringham in order I mean to do all in my power to assist him.' She gestured at the paper-littered floor. 'A great many of these bills are still unpaid. It would be most unfair to leave them!'

The Beau smiled. 'I wonder you scruple, my dear! He has funds enough.'

'I daresay,' she returned, frowning, 'but I do not mean to let him pay for such things as the quails we had for dinner last Sunday, and the tallow candles Mrs Carter uses in the kitchens! These things must be sorted, and it is for me to do it, particularly since he has been good enough to let us remain here until our house is ready.'

The Beau raised his brows. 'Your house? Forgive me, cousin, but this is a piece of good fortune I was not aware of.'

Repressing her irritation, Alicia said: 'Gareth retained the Dower House for our use.'

'Indeed!' The Beau seemed surprised. 'I must admit, my dear Alicia, that that is a piece of fraternal affection I had not counted on! That he even remembered your existence seems to me remarkable.'

'Well, it is a good thing for us he did,' Alicia answered, rather shortly, 'or we should have found ourselves without a feather to fly with! As it is I am in a quandary about how we are not to outrun the constable completely! We have the house, but it is in such poor repair I know not how we are to pay for it!' She looked frowningly at her cousin and then said: 'I do hope, Gregory, that that is not why you are come! For if it is I tell you to your head that it is a wasted visit!'

He looked hurt. 'Alicia, do I understand you correctly?'

'Well, I think you might, since as far as I can remember your visits here have either been requests for money or to escape your creditors!'

His lips curled. 'Fair and far out, cousin! However, you are well aware, I know, that those visits have always seemed most attractive to me.'

She did not misunderstand him, but it was not a line of conversation she wished to pursue, so she turned her back and said: 'I wish you would say how long you wish to stay, Gregory. It is hardly fair on the Major to be forced to accommodate you! Indeed, I wonder that he did not turn you away!'

'He could not do that, I believe, his honour would not allow it.'

She glanced up at him, remembering suddenly that the Major had said they knew each other. 'Gregory, what do you know of Major Harbury?'

His eyes slid sideways to hers and he moved in a leisurely way to dispose his length in a worn, chintz-covered armchair. 'Not a great deal. We have played cards, on occasions, at Watiers, and I have met him, once, at Almack's. Beyond that I know only that his brother is Lord Harbury, and lives in—Derbyshire or Leicestershire, I believe. I cannot admit, my dear Alicia, to any great interest.'

'No, I suppose not.' She was frowning, and thoughtful. Kenyon watched her in silence for a minute or two. 'Gregory, how had he that scar, do you know? Was he in the war?'

Beau Kenyon sighed. 'So I understand. He returned when he lost the eye.' He looked curiously at her. 'Why do you ask?'

'Oh, I don't know, something about him when I asked him about it. Nothing probably.'

'My dear Alicia,' her cousin said, 'if there is something amiss I wish you might tell me! After all, who should you turn to but me?'

She eyed him with dislike, already regretting the thoughtlessness of her disclosure. 'Anywhere, I should imagine! When you lift a finger to help anyone but yourself I shall be quite dumbfounded.'

'Really, cousin, this is most unjust!' he complained, in an injured tone. 'Have I not journeyed all the way from London to see how you do?'

'I don't know,' she said, returning his hurt look with a grave one. 'You never even as a child, did anything without good reason. I find it very hard to believe that pure altruism has brought you here now.'

He smiled enigmatically and laid his finger-tips

together, his elbows resting on the chair-arms. The expression he gave her seemed peculiarly cunning.

Alicia repressed a shudder. 'Gregory, if you have nothing to say to any purpose I do wish you would go away! I have so much to do, and you are only delaying me!'

His lips curled. 'My apologies, fair Alicia!' He rose carefully, examined the perfection of his pantaloons, and sighed. 'I wish I might persuade you to confide in me, you know. If there is something troubling you I might, perhaps, be able to overcome the habits of a lifetime and assist you.'

'I doubt it,' Alicia, muttered, turning away.

He contemplated her gravely for a moment. 'Dear coz, you have a poor opinion of me, I know, perhaps merited. I am aware I have done little in the past to warrant your good regard. However, if I might be of service to you—' He paused, and then said, as though reluctantly: 'There is the matter of Gareth's death, of course. It was never properly explained, was it?'

She turned now, and frowned. 'What mean you, Gregory?'

'Nought, I daresay. Perhaps the story of his fall satisfied you.'

'Of course! Why should it not! Do you consider it a lie?'

'No, no, if you do not! I am glad it is not that that troubles you.'

'Oh Gregory, why must you be so provoking? I do wish you would go away!'

He bowed and pressed one stiff reluctant hand to his lips. 'Your servant, my love. Pray forgive me for disturbing you.'

She nodded curtly, and waited until the door clicked

shut before returning rather abstractedly to her task. But her concentration was gone. The Beau had disturbed her more than she had realised, and she now discovered that the manner of her brother's death had perplexed her from the first. She had received but the vaguest account from her young brother on his return with Gareth's body, and had forborne to press him. Mr Avery had been rather more forthcoming, but even he could not conceal the fact that there were several gaping omissions in the story, and that those persons present had been unable to agree about what had actually happened. At the time she had barely thought about it; what mattered it, after all, since nothing could change the fact of Gareth's death. *Now*, however—she stopped, appalled at herself. What was she doing, even thinking along such lines? It was not like her to listen to Gregory. Had he not always tried to make mischief whenever he could? She remembered when he had told her lies about her brothers when they were children, how she had believed him and let them hurt her. Was she not doing the same now? Was he not merely trying to make trouble between herself and the Major, who had, after all, been more than kind to them? She gave herself a mental shake and addressed herself with renewed concentration to the task before her.

On leaving his cousin Gregory descended once more with leisurely steps to the drawing room. In his absence both Kit and the Major had disappeared, and he frowned for a moment before turning and heading for the library. The Major was, as he had hoped, quite alone, and glanced up with a flicker of interest when the Beau entered.

'Kenyon,' he said, rising from the wing-chair he had drawn to the fire. 'Will you take brandy? It is some of my predecessor's, I believe, but not a bad one.'

Beau Kenyon curled his lip. 'If it is that my Uncle laid down it will be quite fine.'

'Indeed! He was a connoisseur?'

'To some extent. He certainly never paid any duty on it.'

'Hmmm.' The Major was pouring the golden liquid, and now glanced up at his guest. 'There must be a deal of smuggling in these parts.'

The Beau took the glass and examined the brandy in it. 'So I believe, though I myself take little interest.' He sipped at the liquid, and the harshness of his expression softened a little as he savoured it. 'Certainly some of my Uncle's cellar. He had an unfailing instinct for a good vintage.' He set down the glass and contemplated the Major as he stood beside the fire. 'My dear cousin Alicia will have it I have been very inconsiderate in foisting myself upon you.' He raised a hand to silence the Major. 'No, she is quite correct. The truth is, Major, so confused were the rumours that reached me that I could not be easy until I had seen for myself how the land lay.'

'I see. And how does it lie?'

The Beau smiled. 'I find my cousin is a very fortunate young woman. Anyone else, I am sure, would not have scrupled to send them to the rightabout.' He paused, and caught up the glass again. 'And the matter of the Dower House. I own, I had not thought my dear departed cousin capable of such foresight.'

The Major shrugged. 'I know nothing of it. It would seem to me to be a plain case of brotherly concern.'

'Would it indeed?' returned the Beau, sneering slightly. 'You might in truth say you knew nothing of the matter, and I'll wager none of the other players had any notion of it, least of all my thoughtful cousin!'

The blue eye contemplated him gravely. 'I do not catch your meaning.'

'Come now, Major, you are not such a whopstraw, I am sure! I believe this is some scheme you have concocted, you and Avery, perhaps, in an attempt to be kind to the bereft relations! Well, I tell you to your head, sir, that I do not care for such generosity! If anyone is to help my cousins it should be me.'

Major Harbury contemplated him coldly. 'I do not understand what you are suggesting. The Dower House was retained, I suspect, for Kenyon's own use should he fail to repurchase, and as such passes directly to his next of kin.'

'So you would have us believe. I, however, am not so easily taken-in.'

'I see. You have communicated your suspicions to your cousins, I deduce.'

'Not yet. I wished to see what you might say on the matter.'

'I have nothing to say. The matter does not even concern me. However, might I suggest that there is nothing to be gained by divulging your suspicions? They are sorely tried as it is.'

'So I have observed,' returned the Beau, his thin lips curling a little. 'I have just left my dear Alicia positively surrounded by bills, which she is attempting to leave in some order for you. She seems quite overwhelmed by the kindnesses you have shown them.'

'I have done very little, no more than anyone in my position must have done.'

'It might seem so to you, and I grant that it does to them. However, to an impartial observer, such as myself, it cannot but seem decidedly strange.'

'Forgive me if I say that I cannot conceive what business it is of yours.'

The Beau sighed. 'With their elder brother dead their affairs are very much my concern.'

'Miss Kenyon does not seem to think so.'

'Perhaps not, but then my young cousin was always hotheaded. I fear she does not love me overmuch. However,' he continued, raising a hand, 'that is of little consequence. What is apparent to me is that you had somehow contrived to worm your way into the child's confidence, and since I must now be considered as responsible—'

'I thought there was an Uncle Henry, who would now be that, the one who is "as fat as a flawn".'

'—I feel it my duty to demand what you mean by them,' concluded the Beau, ignoring the Major's interruption.

Andrew Harbury could not repress a smile. 'What should I mean, Kenyon? As far as Miss Kenyon is concerned I am sure she will tell you that my behaviour has always been quite decorous, and even Christopher would have to own that I have regarded his—tantrums with the utmost tolerance.'

The Beau raised his chin. 'Tantrums?'

'Nothing to speak of. The boy was merely distressed at losing the house.'

'As well he might be! Doubtless he considers you very much the interloper. I must admit, I find it hard myself to regard you as anything else!'

Andrew smiled, and said nothing.

'But tell me, Major,' the Beau continued, 'you were present, I believe, when my poor cousin met his end. I should be very grateful for your account of how he died.'

'There was no mystery, that I am aware. It was quite widely reported.'

'Perhaps so,' the Beau said, his lip curling. 'However, I should prefer to hear it from a witness.'

The Major shrugged. 'As you wish. Kenyon had been drinking far too much, is the sum of it. I went onto the balcony to blow a cloud so as not to offend the company. Kenyon came to find me, apparently under the impression that I had made my purchase by foul means. Just what he had in mind I know not. Suffice it to say he was in belligerent mood. He took a swing at me, which I avoided. The force of it was sufficient, in his drunken state, to carry him over the balcony onto the pavings. He broke his neck.'

'Hmmm. I understand no one saw exactly how it happened.'

'Radley came out in time to see him overbalance. He confirmed that I was too far from him to have delivered any blow.'

'But no one saw the swing he took at you.'

'No.'

'That is most interesting! Do you know, Major, I am quite delighted to have had this little cose with you!'

'If you intend to make mischief, Kenyon, let me tell you you are wasting your time. My account was not in dispute.'

'No.' The Beau considered him, taking snuff in a leisurely manner. 'Perhaps that is a pity.' He carefully dusted his sleeve and returned the box to his pocket. 'It is an unfortunate business, nevertheless, you will agree.'

'Certainly. Which is why I am concerned to do as much as I am able to assist his brother and sister.'

'Hmmm. Well, we have already discussed that, so I need not again voice my opinions on that subject.' He sighed, and stretched one elegant leg before him. 'I wonder if I was mistaken in not donning mourning?' he murmured, considering the perfection of his biscuit-coloured pantaloons. 'It is true my dear Alicia was not pleased. It is too late now, however. To change my mind would be to admit to error.' He set down his brandy glass and rose carefully. 'Well, Major, I will bid you goodnight. I regret that I shall be unable to make a long stay on this occasion, but I believe that my business might be speedily concluded.'

The Majór nodded absently, and watched frowningly as the Beau took his leave. Moving slowly to the brandy decanter he refilled his glass. Unless he was much mistaken he had at last found his man.

# CHAPTER
# SEVEN

IT was with some impatience the following morning that Christopher Kenyon waited for his cousin to receive him. He rose betimes, arriving downstairs to swallow a few mouthfuls of ham before pushing away his plate. His haste was wasted, however, since the Beau never appeared before midday, and had no intention of submitting to the importunate demands of his young cousin to see him earlier. Kit was forced to kick his heels in impatient inactivity throughout the morning, and when he was finally admitted could barely wait for the valet to withdraw before he exclaimed impetuously: 'Upon my word, Greg, this is beyond all things great! I did not expect you to receive my letter even before today!'

'No more did I,' responded the Beau, inhaling snuff with care.

Kit frowned. 'Then how came you here?'

Gregory Kenyon looked up, faintly surprised. 'My dear coz, did I not tell you? In answer to your sister's letter. Most affecting. I could not resist.'

'But I thought that was all a hum! You mean she truly wrote to you?'

'Indeed she did, and you should be grateful, my dear Christopher, since it has brought me to you rather in advance.'

'But how did you decide to come? Did Ally ask you? Herringham is no longer ours, you know.'

The Beau sighed wearily. 'That, my dear Christopher,

is plainly evident. Unfortunate, is it not? All for no-thing!' He raised his eyes to regard his cousin mocking-ly, and then shut the delicate Sevres snuff box with a snap. 'As for how I came here, my dear Christopher, I am not a fool, whatever you may think! When I returned to London Gerande was gone, there was a vast hue and cry, but the news of Major Harbury's presence was sufficient, I fear, to send me—er—hot-foot to the res-cue.' Leaning back in his chair he regarded his cousin quizzically. 'Where is my friend?' he asked conversa-tionally.

'In the tunnel.'

The Beau raised his eyes to heaven, but said merely: 'Is he content?'

Kit looked uncomfortable. 'Well, actually, not really. That is why I'm glad you've come. Greg, he's a devilish rum card, you know. I can never tell what he's thinking, except that it's generally wicked! I've never met such a cold-hearted customer before.'

'He is the best,' the Beau said shortly. 'I had better see him.'

'Yes, but I say, Greg, what about the Major? I know he suspects, and his batman follows me everywhere.'

'He's an agent, of course. Surely you saw that?'

'Well, of course I did,' Kit answered, irritated, 'but I did wonder just how much he knows.'

'Everything, I should imagine,' the Beau responded calmly.

Kit blanched. 'Good God!' He felt behind him for a chair and sat down. 'What should we do with him?'

The straight dark brows were raised gently. 'My dear Kit, must you ask such a question?'

The young man flushed. '*Kill* him? No, Greg, I shall not!'

'Keep calm, Christopher. You need do nothing. I

shall oblige, or our friend, Gerande.'

'No!' replied Kit explosively. 'You shall not! How could we explain it?'

Gregory Kenyon smiled slightly. 'Dearest coz, we are not so clumsy! An accident, is all. A fall over the cliff, perhaps.'

Kit regarded him in mounting horror. 'How can you talk so coolly? It is a man's life!'

Struggling with his patience Kenyon replied: 'Do you not realise? He would do the same for you! And think no more of it than Gerande.'

Stupidly, Kit stared at his cousin, the colour draining from already pallid cheeks. Slowly he shook his head. 'No,' he said.

Kenyon sighed. 'Dearest Christopher, must you be so obtuse? I daresay such naivety is quite becoming, but oh! so out of place!' He smiled. 'Besides, my dear, think of Herringham. A forged will—the merest suggestion!— and it is yours once more!'

Kit forced himself to look at his cousin. 'And Alicia? What of her?'

The Beau shrugged. 'It is unfortunate, of course, that she is here. I wonder if we could tell her? You will naturally not care to kill her also?' Interestedly he watched as Kit sprang from his chair, his formerly grey face now scarlet with rage.

'Good God!' he cried, starting forward with his fists clenched, 'is there nothing you would not do?'

A smile flickered at the corner of that thin mouth. 'Very little,' he replied, unruffled. 'However, I believe she might be spared.'

Kit, who had been standing threateningly over his cousin, his fists clenched, relaxed slightly, but said: 'Not if Gerande has his way!'

Beau Kenyon sighed. 'He will not waste his talents,'

he said languidly, carefully examining his breeches. 'Besides, he will do as I tell him.'

Kit laughed harshly. 'I wish he might, but you do not know him, Greg!'

The Beau looked up in some surprise. 'I do not need to, Christopher,' he said.

Kit shook his head. 'It is not as simple as you think. I believe he has information on him. He signified as much, and said the Military were after him.'

The Beau sighed and stood up carefully. 'I suppose I had better see him,' he said, when he had assured himself that no crease marred the perfection of his knee breeches. 'Collins, my coat!' His eyes fixed on nothing in particular the Beau waited with an expression of intense boredom as the manservant hastened from the dressing room, bearing with great care a treasured garment of olive superfine, embellished with large silver buttons. Kit watched with growing impatience as the Beau eased himself gently into the coat, and with difficulty repressed an exclamation as his cousin turned to the mirror, and, with painful slowness, adjusted the intricate folds of his cravat. Ready at last, however, he turned to his young cousin, signalling with a careless finger to his man to open the door.

The tunnel was very dark after daylight. The steps leading towards the chamber were unlit, and until the bottom was reached barely a flicker of light reached them from the chamber beyond. With care Beau Kenyon picked his way in the darkness, grimacing as the jutting rock inadvertently caught his sleeve.

The man in the chamber did not at first look up. He was seated, as always, at the table, a blanket about his shoulders, cards spread before him. The two had come within a few feet of him before he sighed and raised heavy eyes. These surveyed the two calmly, rested for a moment on the Beau, and were then lowered once more to the table.

'This is my cousin, Gregory Kenyon,' Kit said, his tone betraying his nervousness.

'I hope, sir, that you intend to take me to France,' said Gerande, not raising his eyes again from the cards.

Beau Kenyon surveyed him. 'I shall,' he said eventually, 'after I have dealt with our little problem here.'

'I trust you know how to do so.'

Kenyon smiled slightly. 'I know, but I might need your aid.'

The Frenchman looked up now, his dark eyes glittering in the light of the candle, and for a moment the two men surveyed each other. 'I shall assist, if it will precipitate my departure.'

'My thanks, I regret you have been thus inconvenienced.'

'Do not regard it. What have you in mind? I am anxious to be gone.'

'Something simple, my friend. I will bring the Major to the tunnel. We may bind him and leave the tide to do the rest.'

The dark eyes glittered. 'And if the body is found?'

'There will be papers on him, incriminating him. The government will think their plans are still safe, while he will be condemned as a traitor. However, the tides are so treacherous, so unpredictable, it is possible he will not be found at all.'

The Frenchman nodded, and seemed to lose interest once more.

'Greg,' said Kit suddenly, coming forward out of the gloom, 'just how are you planning to get the Major down here? He'd not be an easy man to fool, I'll warrant.'

The Beau smiled a little. 'Dear Christopher, do not concern yourself with such things! We will take care of the Major. That should be sufficient for you.'

'I suppose so,' said Kit uneasily, 'but if only there were some other way! Are you sure there is not?'

'No, coz, there is not,' replied the Beau, the sudden sharpness in his tone betraying his irritation. 'Merely be certain you are ready to leave when all is completed. There can be no further delays.'

'Leave?' echoed Kit, looking startled. 'Am I not to stay?'

'I think you had better come. Your dear sister also.'

'But I had planned to stay! There is so much to do!'

'You will come, Christopher. Now, if you please, we will return to the house. I have much to prepare.'

Kit hesitated for a moment, and then, with one glance at the man who sat, his head bent over the table, he followed his cousin out of the chamber into the brilliant light of day.

Alicia awoke very little refreshed. She had retired to bed, convinced she was exhausted, only to find, once there, that sleep was very far away. Not only was her mind so full of accounts that she was perpetually adding up figures, but even these calculations were disturbed by two things—the Major's shadowed, but smiling countenance, and Gregory's hooded, glittering eyes. Try as she would she could not feel quite easy about her cousin. She had never trusted him—in trouble he would be the last person to whom she would turn—and now she found him perfectly repellent. She had been wont to accept his mocking ways—he was Gregory, and one expected such from him. Now, however, he seemed more full of poison than she could remember, more bent on some unknown devilry than she had ever before known him. If only Kit were not such a stranger! But it was weeks, now, since she had felt easy in his company. The one whom she trusted and loved most of all in the world had made her eye him askance, and consider all his actions and words as if he were her enemy. Then there was the Major, who, by some inexplicable cunning, she was sure, had inveigled his way into her affections, making her regard with kindness someone she should properly loathe. She thought about his one-eyed, comical expression, and smiled. How strange to remember that it had only been such a short time ago that she had regarded that eye-patch with horror, instead of sympathy. These thoughts led her back to Gregory, who had been trying, she was sure, to poison the friendship she had with the interloper. What, she wondered, could he possibly hope to gain by such an achievement? Was it merely his love of mischief, or was he prompted by some other purpose? With such thoughts as these keeping her mind active, Alicia slept poorly, and awoke to find herself far from resolved about any one thing.

As she always did when confused, Alicia sought her tree trunk that morning, having satisfied herself that there was no one about either to perceive her or to interrupt. Her mind muddled, it was some little while before she realised that the trunk was vastly uncomfortable that day, and, indeed, that the whole atmosphere of the woods was one of unease. Why did she suddenly feel so cold? The day was clear, the sky pale blue and sparkling. Doubtless a breeze had swept across the valley from the sea, and she looked down from her perch to see if the leafless branches were stirring.

In summer she would not have seen them. The green leaves, shifting and stirring, would have blotted them completely from her sight. Even now her eyes could barely see them, moving as they were like two black strokes among the black stripes of the branches before her. She knew at once that it was Kit and her cousin. They were quite indistinguishable, but the rapid way in which they skirted the shrubbery wall and disappeared around the corner told her it would only be they.

She made her decision in an instant. Scrambling up and hastily grabbing her shawl she was hurrying down the hill as she had hurried so many times before, but borne this time not by delight and wonder but by the certain knowledge that she would not have long. If the servant were still there she would have no time whatsoever, but she could hope that he had finished, and had retired to do whatever valets did when their presence was not required. Clean boots or press jackets, she vaguely supposed.

She was really getting used to running across this lawn, she thought, as she gathered her skirts and hurried through the grass. Her dress flapped, wet and clinging, against her ankles, soaking her shoes and stockings, sticking itself to her legs. She barely noticed it as she hurried across the ruts of the drive and up the steps into the house.

How lucky that there were so few servants! She was through the hall and up the stairs without anyone seeing her, and hurrying, a little breathless, along the passage towards the room her cousin had been allotted. Outside the door she paused, gulping air into her lungs, composing herself before knocking smartly on the door. There was no answer. A surge of excitement set her scalp tingling as she turned the handle cautiously and pushed open the door, the slight creak it made resounding loudly in her ears. Once inside, with the door closed again, she felt suddenly at a loss. Impulse had carried her thus far, but now she was here, just what she should search for eluded her. Taking a breath she moved away from the door, having decided to search methodically all

items of furniture in the apartment. It proved to be a
long task. Her cousin had brought so much with him he
seemed to be expecting to stay six months, and Alicia
was amazed at the quantities of snowy linen that had
been laid with loving care in the drawers. Coats, too,
were in abundance, each, she could tell, fashioned to the
latest mode by a tailor of the first stare. Boots, the gloss
on which she had not realised could be possible, stood in
regimented rows on the floor of the wardrobe, so that
Alicia began to wonder how her cousin should ever find
occasion to wear them all. And yet nothing of interest
could she find. Carefully she had searched, ensuring all
the time that nothing was disturbed, no neck-cloth
creased to show there had been an intruder. Nothing,
however, was to be discovered. Nonplussed, she perched on the end of the bed and surveyed the room,
looking for something that might have escaped her
notice. It was obvious, really. She almost laughed as she
thought of it. Standing up, she moved round to the head
of the bed, and, lifting the pristine cover, slid her hand
cautiously beneath the pillows. A pistol was there, hard
and cold against her searching fingers. Even as her hand
touched it she knew what it must be, and with great care
drew it out. It was long, but light, beautiful, too, she
admitted, with silver mountings. Gingerly she handled
it, not knowing whether it was loaded or not, safe, or
not. Of course, there was no reason why Gregory should
not be armed, or hide his weapon beneath his pillow, but
nevertheless it did seem odd to Alicia that he should do
such a thing on a simple family visit. Naturally, many
men now went abroad armed. The roads were notorious
for highwaymen, and in London a man was a fool who
did not carry protection of some kind. Nevertheless
Alicia felt that something had been proved by her
discovery, that Gregory had not come to Herringham

purely in a spirit of benevolence and concern.

A slight noise behind her made her turn her head. Her cousin stood in the doorway, his eyes alive with interest, a smile hovering on the thinness of his lips. Alicia, frozen where she stood, watched with a strange fascination as he moved, almost cat-like, into the room, and shut the door quite soundlessly behind him.

'My dear Alicia,' he said, his tone mocking her, 'what an honour this is! How sorry I am that I was not here to greet you! But I see you have been making yourself at home.' As the colour rushed into her face he moved around the bed to where she stood and gently removed the weapon from her slackened grasp. 'A pretty piece, is it not? One of a pair, cousin, as I fancy you must have determined. Duelling pistols, in fact. They came in a particularly fine leather case. I suppose I am remiss not to use it. Incidentally,' here his eyes flickered to her face and away again, 'you were really quite lucky. It is ready loaded, you know. But perhaps you realised that.' He looked at her with an expression of cool enquiry and she felt her already high colour mounting.

'I know this must seem strange to you, Gregory, but—'

'On the contrary, my sweet cousin, it is not strange at all. In fact, I am desirous of a little chat with you. Shall we sit down?'

As if she had no will of her own Alicia allowed herself to be led to the window seat, and felt herself gently pressured into sitting. Her cousin seated himself beside her, so close that his boot touched her leg. It was with difficulty that she refrained from flinching. She felt peculiarly frightened.

'You must not think, Alicia dear,' her cousin was saying smoothly, 'that I shall misinterpret your presence here. I shall not. I know exactly what you were doing, and in a sense I am glad, since it makes my task so much the easier.'

'What do you mean?' Alicia forced herself to say.

The smile hovered again. 'It is concern for your brother, is it not? Pure, sisterly affection? Of course it is! You are too high-principled, my sweet, to search people's rooms out of sheer curiosity. I know this, and therefore I am not angry with you.' He smiled at her and patted her hand, and Alicia decided at once that she preferred him frowning. 'So let us come to the point, shall we? Yes. Clearly, my sweet, you do not trust me. Very well. Perhaps I do not deserve trust, since I have come to this splendid house for reasons quite other than I gave you. But so much you have guessed, I know well. Your dear brother, impetuous lad that he is, gave thus much away.' The Beau sighed. 'I wonder whether I was right to enlist his aid? I had always thought him a steady lad, but this latest business—Ah, well, you cannot be interested in *that*.'

'Gregory, enlist him in *what*?' Alicia managed to ask hoarsely.

The brown eyes widened. 'Alicia, my love, can it be that you have not guessed? And you know your brother so well!' He sighed again, and began searching his pockets. 'Now where is my snuff box? Can it be that Collins forgot to transfer it? Surely, surely not! Ah no, here it is! I have maligned the poor fellow!' Carefully he flicked open the Sevres snuff box, placed an infinitesimal pinch on the back of his hand, and inhaled, carefully. 'Now, where were we? Ah yes. Do you mean to tell me, Alicia, that you have not guessed?' He waited for a reply, but Alicia was speechless, staring at him in wide-eyed alarm. 'Hmm,' said the Beau, considering her a moment, 'perhaps I was wrong to involve the family. However, it is done now, so I must make the best of it.

Alicia, my love,' here he patted her hand again, 'I am naturally a Government agent. Naturally. I have enlisted your brother's assistance in a matter quite vital to your country's safety. Are you following me, Alicia?'

He spoke sharply, and she started. 'You are saying . . . you say that Kit is working for the Government? The *English* Government?'

Her cousin looked mildly surprised. 'Of course! Did you not guess it? My apologies, dear Alicia! I had thought you possessed the truth!'

Alicia seemed to have difficulty in mastering the implications of her cousin's statement. 'You say that Kit is working for the *Government*?' she repeated stupidly. 'You mean he is an agent of the *British*?'

The Beau nodded patiently. 'Exactly. At least, not fully an agent, not yet, but he will be shortly, if all goes well.'

Alicia forced her eyes to focus on the face so near to her. 'And you, Gregory, what are you?'

He smiled slightly. 'I? Now I am an agent. I have been for several years, and I hope I have managed in that time to perform some trifling service for my country.'

'And Kit has been helping you?' For some reason Alicia still seemed to find this explanation hard to accept.

The Beau nodded patiently. 'I needed a house somewhere on the coast, a base, where British agents could be safe before being transported to France. Where else should I look than to my second home, especially since I knew my dear cousin Christopher was so in need of assistance in a—er—financial field.'

Whatever is the matter with me? thought Alicia desperately. Why don't I believe this man? 'You have been using Herringham as a *base*?'

The Beau nodded. 'Yes indeed. You should be very

proud of your brother. He made no demur at all. In fact, everything had been working wonderfully well, until now.'

'Now?' echoed Alicia, filled with forboding.

'Yes. Poor Christopher. He scarcely knew what to do! His home taken over, his brother killed, all when he was expecting a man from London at any moment! Imagine, then, his consternation to find the enemy present in his own house!' The Beau paused dramatically, covertly examining his cousin's face from beneath lowered lids.

'The Major an enemy agent?' She seemed quite hor-ror-struck, he thought, interestedly. 'No, and no! It cannot be, it can't!'

Her cousin smiled sympathetically. 'It is difficult to believe, I know. Doubtless he was most plausible, clev-er, too, I expect.'

'No,' said Alicia stupidly. 'I won't believe it.'

'My dear,' said the Beau patiently, 'it is quite plain. Do you not see it? Of course you are angry that he has deceived you, that is most natural. Now, however, he will deceive you no more.'

Slowly Alicia began to collect her thoughts. 'Please, Gregory, let me think. You have made this all very sudden, you know. I must think about it.'

'Of course.' The Beau smiled kindly on her, releasing her hand from the grasp in which he had been holding it for some little time. Agitatedly she stood up, and he watched interestedly as she began to pace the room.

It was all too obvious. Alicia saw that at once. Why, then, could she not accept it? Why was she more ready to believe that her brother had betrayed his country than that the Major had? It was preposterous! *She* was pre-posterous! She must be going mad, even to think of making such a choice. The Major before her brother? No! It was so obvious, too. He had told her so himself, had he not? Had he not said, so plainly, that very first evening—only six days ago, she realised incredibly— 'Miss Kenyon, what would your reaction be if I told you I was an intelligence agent?' How clear it all was, to be sure! Why she could even remember how he had looked when he had made that incredible statement, as if it were the most natural thing in the world, she recalled, an unconscious chuckle escaping her. And now, could it really be true? She had not, seriously, for a moment considered that it might in fact be true. And yet, had he not told her so several times? Yes, she answered herself at once, and also that he was a deserter, and that his father was a highwayman. He had even told Kit, or at least let him believe, that he was a card-sharp. Really, he was a most impossible individual! How was a delicately nurtured female to know what to believe?

But she did know, now, at any rate. Gregory had told her, and it seemed she must believe him, or be content to condemn her brother. This she could not do. Besides, was not Kit's behaviour, his absence, the loss of food and bedclothes, thus all explained? So, the Major was a foreign agent after all. At once a cold chill gripped her, and she found herself thinking of the many little incidents that had seemed so trifling at the time. He had been so anxious to help, so willing to house her while their house was set in order, exerting himself in every way to assist them. So interested had he been in Kit's troubles. No wonder, now, about that! Oh, how he must have laughed at her! She had played right into his hands! And then there was Gareth's death, and the purchase of the house. Kit had said the Major was a card-sharp. If they had known the house was used as a base how easy it would have been to have arranged for him to win! People of that sort would be at no loss for such skills. Gary had always been short of money, had loved gamb-

ling. So little regard he had had for his heritage, too, in
spite of what Kit said. How easy, then, to send one of
their best men to England, to take advantage of a weak
man, how convenient that Gareth was dead, that he
could not verify her fears.

As this thought crossed her mind another, hard on its
heels, relentlessly followed, and she felt obliged to sit
down on the nearest chair. There had always been
confusion about Gary's death, Gregory had already
made her aware of it. There was a peculiar lurch in
Alicia's stomach as her hand flew to her mouth to
prevent the cry that had so nearly escaped. Gareth
*murdered*? Surely, surely not! She knew that no-one had
seen him fall. No one had thought even to question the
Major's story, preferring to believe the story of a reputable officer against the reputation of a gambler and
drunkard. But Gregory had questioned it, had put the
doubt in her mind. Now that she knew the truth it
seemed quite plain to her that the Major had murdered
her brother.

# CHAPTER
# EIGHT

COLLECTED at last Alicia turned to face her cousin. 'Very well,' she said stiffly, 'I accept what you say.'

'I always knew you were a sensible girl, Alicia,' said the Beau, a patronising smile on his mouth. 'Naturally you accept what I say!'

'Well, now that I have,' said Alicia impatiently, 'will you tell me how you intend to get this man to safety?'

'Yes, my sweet, I shall. But first you must come and sit down. Come!' His tone was imperative, and obediently Alicia moved back to the window seat. 'Now that you know the truth it is, of course, so much easier. We shall need you to help us.'

Her eyes flew to his face. 'I? Oh, no, Gregory, I cannot!'

The Beau forced himself to be patient. 'Indeed, my love, you must! Remember it is your country, this England, that you are serving! Then there is Kit! Do you not want to help him? For myself I would not ask it, but for Kit—! Surely you cannot refuse him?'

Even as he said it she knew she could not, but she dreaded the moment when he would tell her what must be done. 'Very well,' she said, thinking as she said so that it would take a stronger person than she was to refuse Gregory.

'Good. Very good. For, you know, our task would be so much harder without your assistance!'

Her heart sinking Alicia forced herself to ask: 'Just

how are you expecting me to help you, Gregory?'

'In a way that will be very easy for you, dearest,' said the Beau with a smile that did not touch his eyes. 'You must win his confidence, get him to trust you completely. Now, that cannot be difficult, surely? Do not ask me to believe that he is not already vastly *epris*, for I have it from your brother that it is so. It would be such a simple thing, would it not, for you to go to him, as you have done so many times before, and say you are so worried about Kit? Only now, of course, you must say more. You are worried, now, about me, too. You have never trusted me, have you, Alicia?' He laughed at her evident confusion, mocking her with his eyes. 'So how easy it will be for you to admit that distrust! You must then get him to trust in you by saying you are frightened Kit has done something dreadful, like betraying his country, and if only there were some way you could help him! I'm sure I need add no embellishments, for you, I am certain, will add them to a nicety. The anxious sister. Quite touching. I only wish I could be present at your performance, but that, alas, is impossible. However, I have complete confidence in your ability, my dearest cousin. With luck, then, *he* will confide in *you*, tell you you are right, Kit has betrayed his country, but that there is yet a way that he might be saved. How, how! you will cry, I will do anything—but I'm sure I need not tell *you* what to say. Then he will tell you, he must, just what he is looking for, only it will be a French agent, of course, not a British one. A French agent, deadly, dangerous, sent to England on some fell mission, and only you, Miss Kenyon of Herringham, can help him to catch the blackguard.'

Alicia felt sickened. He was so clearly enjoying himself, relishing every moment of the deception that Alicia wished there had been some other way, any way, of extricating them all from this dreadful scrape. But even as she thought about it she knew it was impossible. She must trust this man her heart told her to hate. 'And how shall I do that?' she asked him uneasily.

He smiled at her again. He was nearly always smiling, Alicia thought, but she never felt inclined to smile back. 'You will tell him that you know of somewhere where the man could be hidden. The perfect place, untraceable.'

She raised her brows. 'I will?'

'You will. You will say there is a tunnel, where you and your brothers used to play when you were young.'

'A tunnel?' she echoed, surprised. 'There is no tunnel!'

'Oh, but dearest, there is! Did they never tell you, not in all these years?'

She shook her head.

'My word,' he said eyeing her wonderingly, 'how honourable your brothers are! Do you know, I was barely six when I made them swear, on their own blood, that they would never tell a living soul? I had hardly dared hope that they would have preserved their faith, even to this day. I am amazed.'

'Perhaps you are, Gregory,' said Alicia, some of her spirit returning, 'but I wish you would tell me what you are talking of! What tunnel?'

'Forgive me, dearest life! My apologies! In the floor of the old cottage, my sweet, where we used to play.'

'The *cottage*?' she echoed, surprised. 'The old cottage where you all played for so many hours? Good heavens! I always wondered what fascinated you there, but I never guessed it was anything like that!'

'It seems there used to be quite a smuggling trade in the area—I daresay there still is, if only we knew. The tunnel leads from the site of the cottage right down to the beach. It is, in fact, several hundred yards long, as I daresay you can imagine. How it came to be dug I don't know, but I believe the cave on the beach is natural, and so is much of the tunnel. When it gets higher up there are several chambers, used, I imagine, for storing kegs, and these are certainly man-made.'

'And the tunnel is still there?'

He nodded. 'Almost perfect, too, although I believe Kit was obliged to clear a few rocks at one point to make it passable. A small roof-fall, I understand.'

'I hope it's safe,' Alicia remarked thoughtfully.

'Safe enough for our needs.'

Alicia looked dubious, but said: 'And this man, this agent, is in the tunnel?'

Beau Kenyon nodded, his eyes on her face.

'Good heavens!' she exclaimed. 'But is it not damp, and very cold?'

'I believe it probably is,' responded her cousin grave-ly. 'But what else could dearest Kit do in the circum-stances? He must be kept safe at all costs.'

'So that is why he took blankets,' said Alicia, musing-ly. 'Poor Mrs Carter, she would blame Sally for it, and even I could not see why Kit should have taken them!'

Gregory nodded. 'I believe your brother is a little too impetuous, but he intends well. I had not realised, when I requested his aid, how very like our Gareth he is.'

'Yes, isn't he,' agreed Alicia thoughtfully. 'I had not noticed it either, until now.'

She sighed, and seemed about to become distracted, so the Beau said hastily, 'Well, my dear, and will you help us?'

Thoughtfully she regarded him. 'I shall have to, Greg-ory, shan't I? I cannot let Kit die.'

'Good! So, you will tell your Major you know where his agent is hidden, and you will take him there, show him the trap door—it will not matter if you have to search for it a little, my dear. Doubtless it is many years since you were last there—and leave him to go down alone. That is all you have to do.'

Suddenly Alicia looked at him intently. 'And when I've done all this what will you do with him?'

The Beau sighed. 'My dear, I was hoping you would not ask that question.'

'You'll not kill him!'

He shook his head sadly. 'My sweet, this is a bad business. What do you think the Major would have done with Kit, even with you when his purpose was accomplished?'

She looked at him. There was no answer she could give, so she remained silent. Gregory laughed.

'Dear Alicia! Always so trusting!'

'Gregory, is there no other way? Must he die?'

'What would you suggest, dear life? That we set him free onto English society? Or perhaps send him back to London where he can report the activities of our government? He is not without friends, you know, and his brother has influence in high places.'

However have I come to be caught in such a net? wondered Alicia wildly, seeing all the time that her cousin was in the right. There was no way the Major could be saved, and besides, what was she about in even wanting to? Had not the Major been instrumental in her brother's death? Hardening her heart she turned to Gregory and said: 'Very well, Gregory, I shall do as you ask, but do not think you have won my respect, for you have not! I believe I must always have despised you!'

He laughed gently, and caught her hand to his mouth. At the touch of his lips she snatched her hand away as if very contact with him were poison, and he laughed again. 'Dear Alicia! And have I not always loved you?'

She was startled, and did not believe him, but nevertheless there was something in his eyes that made her wish to leave that room as soon as possible. 'There can be nothing else, Gregory, for us to say. I believe, if you do not mind, I shall leave you. I have much to think about.'

He stood up at once, and, every inch a Gentleman of the Ton, conducted her solicitously to the door and bowed her out.

The Major was feeling satisfied. He had just had a visit from a very reliable-looking man called Staines, who had, it transpired, been bailiff at Herringham until dismissed two years previously, as a result of the dwindling Kenyon resources. Andrew had hired him at once, for it was plain that the man knew his business, and had, moreover, been bailiff there for nearly twenty years. Then, too, there had been his daughters, two of them, strong, stout girls, their father said, able and willing to do any sort of work in the kitchens or about the house. The Major had hired them at once, and it only needed Staines to mention a son, a lad of eighteen, mighty handy with horses, for the Major to provide Tom with some much needed help in the stables. He was beginning to think he would enjoy being a man of property, and had it not been for the distressing business on hand he would have felt quite content at Herringham. If only he could resolve the tangle—and at the moment, he had to admit it, it seemed far from likely—he thought he might leave London and stay at Herringham to manage the estate. But before this could even be contemplated he must conclude this business, solve it to the satisfaction of all parties, and save that foolish young man from the scaffold. Just how this was to be achieved when the young man in question was hell-bent on putting the noose about his own neck he could not at the moment

concieve, but done it must be if the Major was to achieve
the object of his desires. He had hardly dared to admit to
himself just what these were. How much safer not to,
when all could yet be lost! Sensing himself to be nearing
dangerous territory he accordingly focused his attention
on the matter before him—a pile of distressingly confused accounts.

Alicia made her way towards the study with lagging
steps. Several times in the relatively short distance from
her chamber she had almost lost her conviction, and it
had taken a very great effort of will to make her continue. She tried to make herself think of Kit, of how
brave he had been, how noble, and of Gareth, neither of
these, perhaps, but at least innocent. The Major was
not. His crime was unforgivable. He had betrayed his
country, had come to Herringham on false pretences,
had taken up residence in *her* home, saying it belonged
to him. The fact that he had not deceived her, that he
had admitted at once what he was occurred to her only to
be dismissed. However kind he seemed it could not
change what he was, nor what she had to do. And yet
how hard it was! How she hated the thought that, to save
her brother, she must lower herself to the level of a
traitor, be as unprincipled as he was himself. With a start
she realised that a door was before her, that her thoughts
had carried her, unknown to the very threshold of her
ordeal, and that she only had to knock to be admitted.
She did so, and a voice at once replied. How strange,
Alicia thought as she entered, that one's limbs could
function unconsciously! She had hardly been aware of
turning the handle on the door, and yet here she was, in
the study, with the Major rising at that moment from the
desk, greeting her with a smile, asking her to sit down.
You mustn't be nice! she longed to say, I'm here to
betray you, to lead you to your death! Aloud she thank-

ed him, and declined the chair. She heard herself speaking calmly, she noticed with surprise, about everyday things, about the garden, the shrubbery, was he going to hire anybody shortly, did he think? She was, of course, avoiding the issue, and it was imperative that she come to the point without delay.

'Actually,' she said with resolution, 'I wanted to talk to you about something else. I don't know why I have been bothering you about the garden, for really it is quite unimportant. Besides, I am sure you will go about things in just the right way without my interference, No,' she said, drawing herself firmly back onto the right track, 'I wanted to speak to you about Kit. I'm so very, very worried! If only you could help me!'

The Major was certainly not proof against beseeching eyes, and the expression in his own as he looked at her was sufficient to make Alicia wish, once more, that she had never agreed to this. It was too late now, though. Already he was at her side, gently insisting that she be seated, pouring her a glass of sherry and watching as she drank it.

'He's been behaving so oddly, Major! Really, you cannot appreciate how changed he is! He was always so calm, so collected, never worried, in spite of his responsibilities. He never seemed to think they were too heavy, although he was so young! Now! He is more like Gareth every day! He will tell me nothing about where he has been, what he has been doing, anything! So what am I to do but think the worst? I have tried, indeed I have, to think of reasonable explanations but nothing fits! And then there is his determination to buy back Herringham, and he actually seems to think he will have funds enough to do it! Major,' here she looked at him intently. 'I am seriously concerned that he is contemplating something dreadful!'

As she said this Alicia felt her heart behaving in a most alarming fashion in her chest. Trying to ignore it she watched the Major who had just left her side and was walking about the room, seemingly deep in thought.

'If only there was something I could *do*,' Alicia went on distractedly. 'I feel so helpless, and yet I'm sure that if he is left to himself he will get into far worse trouble than he is already! Oh Major, what can I do?'

He was regarding her now. 'I don't know,' he said shortly, and then, after a pause: 'To tell the truth I have been wondering that myself.'

Her heart leapt again in her chest, and she was aware of a most unpleasant drumming in her ears, as though that organ had somehow or other conveyed itself into her head. 'And then, I have to admit it, there is Gregory. You have hardly met him, but I know him, and oh, I simply cannot trust him! His influence over Kit has always been unnatural, and I really cannot see just what has brought him here at this time! Of course, there was my letter, but he has never troubled himself about us before, and I really do not see why he should start now!' She regarded him appealingly, and noticed that her words had affected him. She could not decide whether she was glad or sorry.

'You think your cousin might have encouraged your brother in some illegal escapade?'

She turned large eyes upon him and nodded. 'To be perfectly frank, sir, I am afraid they have turned traitor.' As she said the words she eyed him intently, but he neither started nor changed colour. Merely, he continued to regard her with disconcerting intensity.

'Miss Kenyon,' he said at last, leaning against the desk, 'may I trust you? I have something to tell you that must be treated with the utmost confidence. As a matter of fact I wanted to tell you long ago, I hated deceiving you, but truly I had no choice!'

'Major,' Alicia said, eyeing him earnestly, 'if you know something that concerns my brother I beg you will tell me!'

'It is not easy,' he replied slowly, 'and if you had not already a very good idea of the matter I would not tell you now. But it seems you have guessed, though how much—!' He sighed, and ran a hand across his brow. 'I told you before I was an agent. I don't think you believed me, though in fact it is quite true. Oh, not for the French, though I admit I encouraged you to think I was! I work for the British Government. It came about quite by chance. I bought the house, as I said, some weeks ago, not knowing then what I had purchased. I believe someone suspected your brother of being a courier, carrying messages from the coast to London. Nothing particularly dangerous, but enough to worry the Government. When information began to be carried out of England also it was considered more serious. The fact that I had bought the house became known, and it seemed an opportunity too rare to miss. Your brother's death was, to them, fortunate, I fear, since it meant there could be no interference from that quarter. I have friends in the Government, and it was one of these who suggested I might be the perfect man to put a stop to this unfortunate business.'

'And that is all it is?' Alicia asked him. 'The carrying of messages is the sum of it?'

He shook his head. 'I have to tell you that it is not. A more serious passage has lately begun, the transporting of French agents in and out of the country. In one in particular we are interested, a man called Gerande, an agent of supreme skill and deviousness. He has disappeared from London, where he had been watched at all times. I believe he is here, even now.'

'Here?' echoed Alicia, opening her eyes wide, wishing as she did so that all had not gone quite as the Beau had suggested. 'But how can he be here, at Herringham?'

'They have him hidden,' he replied, simply. 'Somewhere there is a place where he can be kept, secure from all chance of discovery. I must find out where. It is my only hope of catching this man before he leaves the country. Once away he will be untraceable, and the information he bears quite lost.'

How convincing he is! thought Alicia wonderingly. Indeed, he almost persuades me to believe him! With an effort she recollected herself. She must not, whatever she did, forget that this man was responsible for Kit's dilemma, must not put her feelings before family loyalty! She must be strong, unpleasant though her task was, and remember that this man had betrayed his friends and his country, and would do so again were he not prevented.

'If only I knew where he might be,' the Major was saying. 'Your brother has been feeding him, I know, and in time I must have found out where he went. However I no longer have time to spare.'

Alicia was frowning. 'There is a place,' she said slowly, 'if only I could find it. I haven't been there since I was young, but Kit and Gregory both knew of it. It would be perfect for what they want.'

'Can you show me?' The Major's eyes were eager and Alicia knew hesitation again.

'Yes,' she said, smiling up at him. 'Do you want to go now? I'll fetch my wrap.'

Hurrying upstairs Alicia refused to let herself think of what she had done, forced herself to ignore the ache in her heart, the constriction in her throat that had, at the last, made speech almost impossible. Think of Kit, of Kit and loyalty, Kit and England, the betrayed agent in the tunnel, of Gareth, dead by the Major's hand, Herringham stolen from them, of Kit and his dilemma. Anything but the Major. That was dangerous. That way lay doubt and confusion. The Major was waiting in the hall and as she approached he opened the door for her to pass through. Don't look at him.

'There used to be a labourer's cottage in the grounds,' she said, finding safety in speech. 'A farm-hand, I believe, or a gardener, perhaps. Anyway, it hasn't been lived in since I was born. We played there a lot, but Papa had it pulled down when Kit fell off the walls and broke his shoulder. The tunnel was in the floor. There have been smugglers around here for quite a while. It leads to the seashore. I'm sure it was always dangerous. It might even have collapsed by now.'

He was walking beside her, towering over her, watching her, too, she sensed, although she dared not look at him.

'Of course, he may not be there,' Alicia said, hurrying on. 'Kit may have decided that it was altogether too dangerous, which wouldn't surprise me, really, when you think of the years it's been there, quite untended. And then, too, it would be so damp! I'm sure I would not like to stay long in such a place!' She gave a little laugh, and was aware of tension in the man beside her. Had she rambled too much? Had she betrayed herself by this hurried speech? The Major was saying nothing, and she knew now, just as she had known before that he was looking at her, that he was staring straight ahead, his eye fixed on nothing in particular.

They had rounded the shrubbery wall now, and a little way ahead she could see the two or three stones that were all that remained of the old cottage. It occurred to her to wonder, now, how it was to be done. How should she get the Major—so large a man!—into the tunnel without entering herself? Would he not suspect? Surely, surely he would! Surely he would sense the trap, turn back, refuse to go on!

He did not. Silently they approached the few relics of the cottage and Alicia, her throat too tight to talk, tears pricking her eyes, began fumbling on the old floor of the cottage for the trap door. For a moment her companion stood motionless, watching her, and then he approached, and began kicking among the branches and dead leaves. Why was he so silent? Could he not speak? Could he not sense how much she wanted to hear his voice, if only to ease the terrible drumming in her own ears.

And then her fingers touched cold metal. She realised as she pushed away moss and leaves that she had been hoping all the time that the trap door would not be found, that she could say she was mistaken, return to the house, forget about it. He was helping her now, kicking away the covering, bending down to grasp the ring firmly in a strong hand. And still he did not speak. Alicia risked a glance at his face. It was unusually grim, the scar standing out white and livid against the sudden harshness of his features. And then suddenly he looked at her, the blue eye hurt, so hurt, pained by the knowledge, reproaching her for what she had done. He had known, always he had known! She longed to cry out, say she could not help it, but a strange constriction was in her throat preventing all speech. And then the trap door was open, lying back on the grass, a gaping hole black before them. He started to say something, what it was she could not tell, for at that moment a man neither had seen came from behind and struck the Major sharply on the back of the skull.

Beau Kenyon caught him before he hit the ground, and, without glancing at Alicia said sharply: 'You did well. Go back to the house and collect your things. I shall not be long.'

She hardly heard him, but turned and stumbled back towards the house, not waiting to see the inanimate form bundled into the blackness. How had she ever thought she could do such a thing and remain guilt-free? It was impossible. She knew it now, and even the recollection that Kit was saved did nothing to salve the ache. She saw, too, *now*, that it was all madness, why did she have to betray him so terribly? Why had the Beau involved her in that dreadful way? Did he have to be lured from the house? Couldn't they have done it there, without all the deception? She knew why, of course, at once. She was involved now, involved as much as Kit and the Beau himself. She was equally responsible with them for a man's death. They had trapped her as surely as they had trapped the Major and she could not now be free. Never would she be free from the weight of guilt, the burden of consciousness that had assailed her as he had regarded her, so calm, so hurt, across the blackness of his own grave.

She had stumbled blindly in the direction of the house; her skirts caught and whipped against her legs, almost tripping her as she ran unseeing through the shrubbery paths, old knowledge carrying her unerringly forward. She had lost her wrap—it had fallen from her shoulders at the tunnel entrance, but she had not noticed it, not did she now notice the wind that was cutting through her gown and chilling her to the bone. And then hands, strong, firm, caught her by the shoulders, stopped her flight, shook her a little. She had not realised she was crying, but became aware now of how wet her cheeks were, and fell gratefully into the arms of her young brother.

He had troubles of his own, but Kit was not proof

against such grief, and found himself strangely torn by something which, his instincts told him, should only irritate. Some of his old strength returned, the strength that had carried a sister and a grief-stricken mother through their hardest trials, and he silently stroked the head that was pressed against his shoulder.

When the sobs had subsided a little and only the occasional shudder ran through her body he said gently, vainly trying to see her face: 'Ally, what has happened? Why are you crying?'

She gave a convulsive sob at his words but raised her head and looked at him. 'Oh Kit! You do not know what he has made me do!'

Her brother stiffened. 'Who, Ally?'

She sniffed. 'Gregory. He has taken the Major.'

For a moment Kit stared at her in stunned silence, and then he said explosively: 'And you let him? Oh Ally, whyever did you do it? Could you not fetch me? I could have done something! Heaven knows what, but do you not realise you have sent a man to his *death*? They are perfectly ruthless, Ally! There is nothing they would not do!'

'Oh Kit, I know, but what could I do? I could not let him kill you!'

'Ally, I am sure he would not! Besides, if he did, it would be no more than I deserve. You do not seem to realise what I have done!'

As he ran one hand across his eyes a cold chill enclosed his sister and she stared at him, horrified as the truth dawned upon her. 'Kit, what was he? Who did he work for?'

He raised his eyes and looked at her wonderingly. 'Ally, he was a Government agent! Surely you knew! He came here after me!'

She could not speak. Brother and sister stared at each

other, realisation coming simultaneously. Kit recovered
first.

'There may yet be time! They were going to bind him
and put him in the cave. Perhaps the tide is not yet risen.'

'Oh, then let us hurry! Do let us!'

'Wait! Let me think. It is not so simple.' For a moment
he frowned, staring at the ground, and then he raised his
eyes to her face, scanning it urgently. 'Ally, I need your
help. We must hurry! Even now they may be ready to
leave! Listen to me. Go back to the tunnel, they'll be
gone by now, and do what you can do for the Major.
There'll be a lamp at the bottom of the steps. There are
fourteen of those. Count them carefully, it's very dark. I
must get to the carriage. Somehow I'll stop them, the
Lord knows how. Ally, you will do it, won't you?'

'Of course,' she said impatiently. 'Only Kit, do take
care! Gregory has a pistol, no, a *pair*, and I'm sure he
would not scruple to use them on any of us!' She moved
away and then, as an afterthought, turned back and
stood on tiptoe to kiss his lean cheek. 'Don't worry,' she
said briefly, 'I know you did it for the best.'

# CHAPTER
# NINE

ANDREW HARBURY could see nothing at all. When he
opened his eye complete blackness surrounded him, so
heavy as to be almost tangible. For a moment he lay still
as consciousness returned to various parts of his body—
all present, he deduced, from the aches that assailed
him. He was lying on his back, awkwardly twisted, his
arms pulled tightly behind him, and bound. His feet
were bound too. With an effort he straightened himself.
He was lying flat now, staring up at where the roof
should be. He lay thus for a few more minutes, and then
rolled onto his face. He was on sand. His hands had been
bound so tightly that they were completely numb, and he
had been unable to determine on what he lay. Now,
however, fine grains were in his mouth, his eye, up his
nose, making him cough, his good eye run. Putting his
weight on his forehead he drew his legs up slowly into a
kneeling position, and was thus able, at last, to sit up.
There was no relief in the blackness. But now he was
aware of a new sensation, and realised he had been
hearing it for some little time without registering it. The
sound of the sea, waves beating against rock. The cave—
he assumed thus much—was dark and smelled of sea-
weed. The sand, too, on which he now knelt, was firm
and damp; moisture had made his clothes almost sodden
while he lay. With a jolt he realised that the tide must
reach this point, and it was necessary for him to make
some move. The question was, whether he should leave

by the sea-entrance, or follow the tunnel backwards in the hope that he should eventually reach the trap-door.

The recollection of his betrayal made him frown, and quickly he pushed the matter from his mind. Better far now to concentrate on escape. With this end in view he pulled tentatively at the ropes binding his wrists. They were tight, chafing painfully as he moved. His boots at least protected his ankles, but it was quickly apparent that this would avail him little. In total darkness he would be unlikely to find any rough edge on which to rub his bonds. Nevertheless he determined on action, and, having listened carefully for several moments he heaved himself to his feet—an awkward matter, one which he attempted several times before succeeding—and began to jump in the direction away from the sea. It would be impossible, he knew, to swim thus handicapped.

He quickly found that jumping with his hands bound was no easy feat. He needed his arms for balance, and several times fell heavily onto the sand as his sense of balance betrayed him. In the dark, too, it was awkward, and more than once he found he did not know he was falling until the ground rose up suddenly to greet him. Nor was it all soft sand. On one occasion he fell heavily onto his side, and a sharp rock caused him to give a genuine cry of anguish as it dug viciously into his hip. It was a consolation, however, that he now had something on which to fasten his energies, and, wriggling himself laboriously into a suitable position he began with pain-staking care to rub at the ropes on his wrists

It was while he was thus engaged, bending all his concentration on this futile task, that the first wave lapped his thighs as he sat. His breeches were already sodden from the sand, but nevertheless the water washing over his legs was icy cold, none the less for being so complete a shock. He had not counted on the tide rising so soon. In his rough calculations he had supposed he would have half an hour at least, but it occurred to him now that he must have lain unconscious for longer than he supposed. Another rush of water roused him with a jolt, running as it did into his boots and soaking his feet.

Experimentally he pulled at his bonds but they appeared little looser, while his wrists had been rubbed raw by his fumbling efforts. More urgently now he rubbed at the rock, unable to determine whether the moisture that ran down his arms as he worked was blood or merely water. The next wave confirmed that it had been blood. It was higher this time, flooding over his legs, and washing his wrists as he sat. The salt in his wounds made him grit his teeth. He did not stop, however. To stop, he knew, would be the end. He could never begin again. Already despair, like a fatal illness, was creeping upwards from his frozen feet and legs, and only dogged determination, he knew, would enable him to survive. With the idea of occupying his mind as he worked he began coldly to calculate his chances of survival in these conditions. Numbness would creep up his body, he supposed, robbing him of the power of movement, and, eventually, of thought. To avoid this he began moving his legs as he lay, trying to preserve some semblance of warmth in his limbs, but the effort was costly, and before very long he gave this up to concentrate once more on his wrists. Already, he discovered, he was no longer feeling the cold of the water that now covered his legs. In a sense it was a relief. More easily now could he bend his rapidly dwindling concentration onto the task of freeing himself. Periodically his efforts were hindered by convulsive bouts of shivering that wracked his entire body, the unconscious efforts, he dimly realised, of that same body to stay alive, to preserve essential warmth.

Gradually a new sensation took him over. He was aware of floating, not simply on account of the water that had risen to his waist as he sat, but as a separate entity, apart from his own body. He seemed to be watching himself, his own futile efforts on the rock now almost completely submerged, and knew then, with sleepy realisation, that this was encroaching death, that without the will to survive body and mind would further part, without the ability, or desire to return. And now, suddenly, his strength so nearly washed away, returned in force, and he began with renewed zest to rub away at the rapidly vanishing rock. Strength flooded his arms, determinedly he counted the strokes in his head, forcing his mind into union with his body. He would not let them part again until death itself took him over.

The water by this time was half-way up his chest. He was aware once more of the absolutely freezing conditions in which he worked, and forced his hands harder onto the surface of the rock. For a moment he could not understand what had happened. His arms hung limply as though all life had drained suddenly from him, and then, with a peculiar sensation of purpose having been taken away he realised he was free. Such had been his concentration that for a moment he did not know what to do, then his senses returned and he bent forward to the bonds at his feet. He could not find them. So numb were his fingers, so chaffed his wrists, that no feeling remained, and although he knew his feet were bound he could not find the knots. For a moment he knew panic. The water now was nearly to his chin. How could he escape with no fingers? Perhaps, indeed, he had no fingers. Perhaps they had dropped off with the cold, as had the fingers and toes of many of his men, cold-stricken in the Peninsular. Once again he forced himself to be rational. Of course he had fingers. It was merely a matter of finding them. Holding his arms above the icy water he brought his hands together, missing several times because of the dark. Experimentally he rubbed them, but it was of little use. He could barely feel them, and the sensation now was that they had swollen to several times their normal size. Of a sudden he knew resignation. Escape was impossible. How strange, then, that at this very moment of acceptance of his fate he should hear a voice, seemingly very far away and above him, calling his name.

For a bemused moment he wondered if it were angels, and then he laughed at this ridiculous notion. For the voice had sounded again, more urgently. Now, indeed, he recognised it, but what was that strange croak that sounded from right beside him? He laughed again, soundlessly, for the croak was himself. He tried again, and again the voice was feeble, unlike his own. She must have heard it, though for she called again, with greater insistence, this time. How strange that it should still seem to come from above him!

Now he was aware of a glimmer of light, so faint, barely reflected on the water that surrounded him. This time he looked up, and above him, high above him, was a lantern. It could only be Alicia.

'Major!' Her voice floated down to him faintly. 'Are you all right? Wait! I'm coming down!'

Still slightly bemused, the Major tilted his head to watch her, wondering as he did so just how she was proposing to come, whether floating, like a bird, her skirts billowing out to support her, or in some other fashion he could not determine.

It was in some other fashion that she came. She had found, after much fevered searching, a rope ladder thrown hastily to one side, its upper end still fastened securely in the rock. She flung it down now, and began to make the perilous descent of twenty feet of sheer rock face. She had had to leave the lantern behind her, perched on a small jutting rock, for her hands were so occupied with her skirts that she could not carry it. As it was the light it threw was so feeble that she could barely see, and once, catching her foot in her flounce as she descended, she only saved herself from falling by grabbing frantically at the bar above her. She could just see the Major below, the pale moon of his face turned up as she descended, oh so slowly, to his level.

The water, when she gained the bottom rung, was a complete surprise. She stepped down into it unknowing, and it washed her legs with icy fingers, dragging her skirt heavily about her knees, and as she reached the Major she saw that only his head remained above the surface. In fact, had he not thrown it back to look at her he would have been almost completely submerged.

'Are you all right?' she said urgently. 'Can you stand?'

'My feet,' he managed, his voice returning, though hoarse. 'I can't untie them.'

Ignoring the water she bent down into the iciness, fumbling for his bonds. His feet had been buoyed by the water as he sat and now floated gently as the tide rose and fell. Sudden panic surged over her as she felt how tightly the knots had pulled, but she forced herself to be calm and began tugging at the ropes. All the time the water level was rising and now the Major was spluttering as he sat. Forcing herself to be calm Alicia attacked the knots again, willing them with her whole mind to grow loose. And they did. Miraculously her fingers found purchase on a small loop and she pulled frantically, untying one knot, and then the other.

'Give me your hand!' she cried desperately. 'You must stand up!'

He knew he must, and, gripping the hand she had pressed into his as tightly as his swollen fingers would allow he drew his legs up slowly beneath him. 'Damn!' he exclaimed, above the level of the water as his knees buckled pathetically beneath him. He tried again, putting more weight than he knew on Alicia's slender arms, hauling himself upright, forcing his legs to bear his weight. Standing now, grasping her arms for support, he gave a shaky laugh.

'My hands!' he said. 'I could never climb the ladder, I've no feeling.'

She grasped them at once. They were ice-cold. 'Put one in your mouth,' she told him. In the dim light he was staring at her. 'Do it, please!' she begged him. 'It will warm it a little.' At that he obeyed, while she took the other between her own and began rubbing it with a certain desperation. Together they stood, thigh-deep in water, each concentrating entirely on this simple object. Alicia, driven on by the memory of her betrayal, rubbed the puffed and frozen hand frantically, willing it to be warm, the life to return.

'Give me the other one,' she commanded shortly.

This one was perceptibly warmer, and as she began rubbing a small pang of hope flickered within her that he might, after all, be able to climb the ladder.

'Are they any better?' she asked him eventually, peering upwards at the pale round of his face.

'A little,' he said, flexing his fingers experimentally. 'I think I might be able to climb now.'

'Thank God!' she exclaimed, relief threatening to find outlet in tears. 'Do let's hurry! I'm sure the tide will get much higher yet!' She groped before her for the rope, found it, grasped it tightly. 'Do you think you ought to go first? While your hands are still a little warm?'

'No!' he said forcefully. 'You must go. At least I am taller than you. Besides, I can keep rubbing my hands until you are at the top. Now go!'

Obediently she turned and fumbled with her foot for the bottom rung. She found it, but it became apparent almost at once that her weighted skirts would be a problem. While still in the water they dragged her down heavily so that to pull herself free of the lapping waves was not simple. Then she had to hold her skirts up with one hand so that she could grope with sodden boots for the next rung, and then pause while she moved her hands upwards. It was far harder than coming down, and she had considered that a task she would not repeat with any degree of pleasure. One rung at a time, it took so long, and all the time she was conscious of the man below her, waiting patiently, watching her, as she proceeded with painful slowness. And all the time, too, the tide was rising! The moon had passed the last quarter, so the tide would not be at its height, she estimated roughly, until about eight o'clock that evening, by which time they would both have been thoroughly submerged. How much further it seemed up the face than it had done to climb down! And then, too, she had thought she would never reach the bottom. When at last her hands touched level rock she was almost exhausted, and hauled herself with a final effort onto the top of the face. Turning she called down to the Major, and positioned herself so that she could see how he fared. He had moved to the ladder now, and she quickly grasped the lantern from its promontory so that he might have all possible light. She could see the top of his head only now. How far away it seemed, barely moving! Now he had glanced up, now he looked away again. Once, her heart in her mouth, she heard the rasp of his boot as his foot slipped from the rung and saw the jerk of his body as his weight fell onto his hands. Then he was steady again, and growing slowly nearer. At last he was near enough for her to hold down a hand to him, but he did not take it, preferring to climb in his own slow, painful fashion. And then he was on the ledge too, face down on the rock, collapsed exhaustedly, his feet still hanging in space. Dumbly Alicia took his arms and half dragged him further to safety as his knees made weak efforts to help her. Then she sat down too, weak alike from tiredness and relief.

Lying there on the rock it seemed easiest to the Major to remain motionless, to let time slip by regardless. With an effort he collected himself, realising the necessity for activity in his frozen state. Already the convulsive shivering had begun again, and he had Alicia now to care for. She was sitting nearby, staring at nothing, and he recognised in her the signs of mental paralysis that had so nearly overcome him so short a time ago. With an effort he dragged himself to his knees and thence to his feet. Bending, almost falling, he sought her hand, pulling her upwards as she had pulled him.

'Come on,' he said shortly. 'You'll freeze to death.'

Unthinkingly Alicia got to her feet, automatically gathering her lantern. She made no protest as the Major took it from her grasp and they set off together back along the tunnel. It sloped steeply upwards, the tunnel being roughly carved from solid rock by unknown hands years before. Generally it was straight, but occasionally a secondary tunnel struck off at an angle, causing them for a moment to hesitate. It was these tunnels that delayed Alicia in her errand. She had spent some time in deciding which was the main tunnel and which led merely to another chamber or dead end. Several times had she cursed Kit for his negligence in directing her. How much easier it was now with a strong arm to guide her, and strong shoulders on which the problem of escape could now rest. In a few minutes they would reach the steps, and then they only had to climb them to be free. Already they had reached the chamber where the Frenchman must have spent those wretched days and nights. She had seen the blankets and the remains of food on her way down.

It was as they traversed this chamber that the first intimations of disaster reached them. A hissing, sizzling noise reached Alicia's ears, and at the same moment she felt the Major stiffen beside her, halting suddenly. He waited a second only before ejaculating 'My God!' and flinging her upon the ground. She cried out in mingled surprise and pain, and then all the breath was squashed out of her as the Major flung himself bodily across her, smothering her head against his chest. And then all hell broke loose. Alicia was aware of a blinding flash from across the chamber and of a terrible, deafening explosion that echoed and rebounded off the solid walls. And then the roof was falling in around them. She felt the Major's body tremble as rocks struck his back, heard him cry in pain.

How long it continued she could not tell. It seemed hours before the last echo of falling stone had died away.

# CHAPTER
# TEN

FOR a moment Kit watched as his sister hurried away, doubt seizing him about the wisdom of such a course. Then he recollected the existence of the Beau's pistol and decided that at least in the tunnel there could be no such danger. Accordingly he turned and started back towards the house.

A carriage was already drawn up before the portico and one or two boxes had been strapped to the roof. At present, however, there was only Tom to be seen, standing at the leaders' heads and murmuring soothingly in their pricked ears. Out of habit Kit gave a nod in response to Tom's forelock pulling and ran lightly up the steps and through the open front door. There was no one in the hall either. He hesitated a moment, undecided, and then crossed with quick, ringing steps to the shabbily carpeted stairs. He was barely half-way up, however, when his cousin appeared at the head and began a leisurely descent.

'Why, coz!' he murmured, seemingly quite unflustered, 'such unbecoming haste! Is aught amiss?'

Kit had stopped and now surveyed the Beau with a crease between his brows. 'No,' he said shortly, after considering the question. 'I thought I had better collect my things since you are so intent on being gone.'

Kenyon frowned fleetingly, and then smiled. 'Do so, sweet Christopher, with all reasonable haste. Our friend Gerande has been delayed long enough, I fear. He grows weary of our company.' He passed his cousin now, but a few steps further and he stopped again, and, turning, said: 'By the by, Christopher, have you seen your sister? I was a little concerned. She seemed quite distraught.'

Kit achieved a careless shrug. 'She is somewhere, I daresay. The fact is, Greg, I'm past caring.' He turned on the words and ran up the last few stairs. The Beau, however, remained as though transfixed, a thoughtful frown puckering his brow. Then he too turned, and proceeded on his way.

Although he had already been some distance from him Kit had sensed his cousin's incredulity, and it caused him a moment's anxiety as he ran along the passage towards his apartment. It was necessary for his cousin to be convinced of his unconcern, but at the moment he needed to concentrate on protecting himself against physical dangers. Of Gregory's pistols he was a little wary, but the thought of Gerande quite unarmed caused a constriction in his throat, and it was with fingers that trembled slightly that he drew his knife from its sheath and carefully fingered the blade. He had had it since childhood, when Gary had given it to him in a fit of careless generosity with the idea that he should skin rabbits therewith. He had not done so, but had retained the knife nevertheless, and had, some months previously, taken it from its resting place to sharpen it on the old grindstone in the stable yard. There had once been an impressive armoury at Herringham, but now all that remained was a couple of old guns, used mainly by Tom on the estate rabbits. Not deeming those suitable for concealment, Kit elected to take the knife, and it was this that he now hid carefully beneath his coat. Moving to the mirror he ensured that no sign was apparent as a bulge in the smoothness of his coat, and, in spite of his worry, grimaced at the sight of himself thus revealed. He had been a fastidious young man, careful of his appearance, but of late it had seemed to matter little how he looked. Not so long ago unpolished boots would have been unknown, but now he seemed rarely to rest long enough for them to be cleaned. He shrugged his shoulders at the carelessly attired young man before him, and turned back to more pressing matters. Pulling an old cloth bag from the depths of a wall-cupboard he proceeded to select at random shirts and cravats and push them into the bag. Since he had no intention of going far it really did not seem to matter what he took, but appearances must be maintained. When satisfied that the bag bulged sufficiently to allay suspicion he glanced rapidly once more around him and then strode quickly from the room.

He found the Beau beside the chaise, his smelling salts already in his hand, supervising the final disposal of his baggage. At the sight of Kit's modest bag he raised his quizzing glass to his eye and surveyed his cousin with one eyebrow raised.

'Doing it too brown, coz!' he murmured softly, a gleam in his eyes. 'However, doubtless you know what you are about.' With that he seemed to forget all about Kit and his luggage, not pausing to see it disposed on the roof of the vehicle, but climbing at once into the shadows of the chaise. Kit, having glanced nervously around for a sight of Gerande, climbed in too, and was at once told he must travel with his back to the horses.

'For we cannot expect Gerande to travel thus, dear coz, can we!' he explained, raising his eyebrows quizzically. 'And I daresay if it were I, I should be quite extinct before even gaining the village.'

It was a matter of indifference to Kit where he sat, but he found the Beau unusually irritating, and sat down in the opposite corner without a word. The carriage was unusually comfortable, the squabs thickly padded and covered with velvet in a delicate biscuit shade, matching exactly, Kit noticed incuriously, the breeches his cousin was just then wearing. He was wondering what had become of Gerande. Alicia had gone alone into the tunnel, and although Kit was reasonably certain Gerande was no longer there it concerned him that he was so tardy in making his appearance.

'Greg, where is the fellow?' he demanded irritably of his cousin. 'Is he not coming?'

The Beau smiled fleetingly. 'Patience, sweet coz, he will be with us directly.'

And to be sure, as though this were his cue Gerande appeared at that moment in the doorway, climbed without a word into the carriage, and seated himself as far as possible from the two of them.

'I suppose we can go now,' said Kit, forcing himself to sit still.

The Beau raised one eyebrow. 'Dearest Christopher, surely we await your sister!'

Kit flushed uncomfortably. He had, in fact, forgotten that she was supposed to be with them. 'She's not coming,' he said shortly, failing perfectly to meet his cousin's eyes. 'She'll have no more of it, Greg, so it's best we leave her.'

The Beau's eyes snapped angrily and he pushed aside the rug he had draped over his knees. To Kit's surprise, however, Gerande laid a restraining hand on the Beau's shoulder and said softly: 'Be calm, my friend. She is well enough.'

Something must have been conveyed in the gentle pressure of Gerande's hand, for the Beau at once relaxed, and disposed the rug again across his knees. 'Very well,' he said shortly, tightly clutching his smelling salts. 'Let us delay no longer!'

The door was closed, and the steps let up, and in a moment they were moving forward down the rutted drive. It was with a sense of inordinate relief that Kit watched the walls of Herringham draw away, and he tried to relax as the Beau's well-sprung chaise passed lightly over the ruts and pot-holes that characterised the Herringham drive. It was as he thus surveyed his retreating home that he saw a small figure run round the house to stand as if perplexed in the carriage-way. It remained thus for a second, and then hurried off in the direction of the stables.

Chegg had been anxious for some little time. He had observed his master's departure with Miss Kenyon and had not considered it worthy of remark. He had himself been unobtrusively observing the activities of the Beau's valet, a person of such top-lofty notions that Chegg had rapidly decided he deserved watching. He had also been on his guard for an appearance of young Mr Kenyon, but this gentleman's behaviour had seemed so erratic, and where he went so complete a mystery that Chegg had decided to follow what promised to be a more profitable line of enquiry. He had observed the packing of the chaise with a little puzzlement. It seemed odd indeed that the fine gentleman should leave so hard upon his arrival, especially since he was, at his own avowel, a poor traveller. However, Chegg had long since desisted in his attempts to understand the Quality, even such highly suspicious Quality as the Beau. It was while he was thus comfortably observing his fellow valet that it occurred to him that it had been an uncommonly long time since he had last seen his master. Seized at once by an uncomfortable and decidedly unwelcome feeling of forboding he had left his post by the window of his master's dressing room and had hurried at once to the library. From there he had proceeded to the study and the front parlour, growing all the time more certain that something was seriously amiss. The disappearance of Miss Kenyon also boded ill, and it was just as he was returning from a futile search of the rose gardens that he heard the carriage move forward down the avenue. At once it was perfectly plain to him what must have happened. The reason for the rapid departure was at once apparent. The Major had of course been rendered insensible and was at that moment being conveyed to some terrible and unimaginable place of execution. He had rounded the house in time to see that the carriage was too far away to be stopped, and, hesitating only a moment to check on the presence of a heavy, but serviceable horse-pistol, he had turned and made off at a run for the stables. He was not sure what good he could do, but he was already feeling guilty at having taken care of his master so imperfectly, and fully intended to rescue him or lose his life in the attempt.

On gaining the stables, however, he discovered unexpected resistance from the boy Tom. These two individuals had taken an instant dislike to each other, and Tom had no intention of surrendering his master's beautiful roan to a heavy handed fellow like his master's batman. He listened stolidly to all the little man's protestations but nevertheless would not remove his hand from the door to the mare's stall.

It did not take Chegg long to realise that drastic measures were needed. Already the carriage would be beyond the Herringham grounds and every second meant greater danger for his master, and less chance of his being rescued. Chegg had not been the champion bruiser in the barracks for nothing. Before Tom realised what was to happen a smart right had been delivered to his jaw and he had crumpled without a murmur where he stood. With a grunted word of apology Chegg grasped his arms and pulled him awkwardly clear of the door. The roan was unsaddled, but with scarcely a thought Chegg had dragged down the heavy saddle and thrown it across the animal's back. Not used to such careless treatment the beast snorted and backed, and Chegg was forced to waste precious seconds on calming the animal. Saddled and bridled at last, however, she was led out into the biting February air, fresh and ready to go. Chegg was a smaller man than the Major, so mounting the beast proved difficult, and he wished he had taken the trouble to lead her to the mounting block. Once seated, the animal needed little encouragement, but sprang forward with a leap, the hooves raising sparks from the cobbles of the yard.

Knowing the Beau's dislike of travel Chegg was a little surprised that the chaise had already vanished from view, and realised with a sinking spirit that he had taken longer than he thought to get the animal saddled and prepared. The beast was willing enough, however, and responded to his demand for speed by stretching out her neck against the wind, and her legs into a gallop. For a while he let her have her way. They passed the lodge gates and headed down towards the village, but after about a mile he reined her back to a gentle canter. How far he would have to go he could not tell, and he had no wish to break the mare by pressing her too hard at first. It was of concern to him that there was no sign of the carriage on the road. He could not imagine that it would head for Coddlington, a village possessed of no more than a few scattered cottages, so London seemed most likely. He determined, however, to inquire in Herringham village, in case it had been seen. The light was fading now; within an hour it would be dark, and then his chances of finding the carriage and his master would be

greatly reduced. On the outskirts of the village he drew
the mare back to a trot in the hope that he might pass
someone of whom he might inquire. The village was
quiet, however, and it was not until he had reached the
green that he saw two ragged children, their hair tangled
and matted, playing in a muddy puddle on the edge of
the grass. At the sight of the large horse they stopped
pushing each other and surveyed the rider with frank
curiosity. Chegg comtemplated them a moment, and
then said: 'Have you seen a coach?'

The older of the two, a boy, with brilliant blue eyes,
considered his questioner a moment, and then lisped:
'Yes! At the Inn!'

Searching in his pockets Chegg found a solitary pen-
ny, which, without thinking, he tossed into the muddy
palm outstretched before him. Then he spurred his
horse once more into a trot and approached the Inn.

There was indeed a coach in the yard. At that moment
ostlers were leading steaming horses from the traces
and it was clear that they had travelled far, a great deal
further than from the Hall. He was about to turn away
when the panel of the carriage arrested his attention. It
was generously coated in mud, and the arms there
displayed were partially obscured. To Chegg, however,
they were so familiar that he recognised them at once,
and, shouting for the ostler he swung himself from the
saddle and strode into the inn.

The sight of a person, clearly a member of the lower
orders of society, calmly marching into the best private
parlour very nearly caused the landlord a spasm, he
explained, rather later, to his wife. With a startled cry he
hurried forward, but he was already too late. The person
had stridden into the parlour, straight into the presence
of the most prestigious person the landlord had entertained since old Mr Kenyon died. With words of apology

already flowing from his lips he hurried after the intruder. As he expected his lordship had risen from his chair, an expression of great puzzlement on his face. But as the landlord's confused apologies tumbled forth the expression cleared and his noble guest started forward.

'Great Heaven!' exclaimed Lord Harbury, regarding the batman as though he were his saviour. 'Surely you are Chegg!'

'Yes, my lord, I am,' responded the fellow gravely. 'And I should be very grateful if you could lend me your assistance.'

The pace set by Beau Kenyon's coachman was not one calculated to agree with his master's constitution. It was a sign of that gentleman's great concern for his important passenger that he had disregarded the wishes of his own stomach and had ordered his coachman to 'put 'em along'. As a result he now sat with his eyes closed, his smelling salts raised almost continually to his face, motionless but for the rocking and plunging of the chaise. For a while all three maintained unbroken silence. Kit observed the passing of Herringham village, idly noticed the scamperings of two urchins in a puddle, and then they were out once more into open country, rattling with some speed along the cliff. Until this moment he had only the vaguest of ideas of how he should stop these men. Even Gregory, grey-faced as he now was, could not be regarded as inoffensive, and he knew that for Gerande nothing was too much for his conscience. He could feel the handle of his knife hard beneath his elbow as he sat, and it brought him comfort, if only a little. He glanced at Gerande, and saw, with a sudden lurch in the pit of his stomach, that the glittering eyes were watching him steadily from beneath the straight dark brows. Gerande had now shaved and washed, presumably this was what had delayed him, but the improvement in his appearance did nothing, in Kit's eyes, to lessen his sinister aspect, and it was with difficulty now that he drew his eyes away from that cold regard. There was no chance, he knew, that Gerande would fall asleep. Although he must have slept little during the past few days Kit sensed that he did not trust him, had never done so, in fact. And such was the man's spirit that he would never sleep while the chance of betrayal existed. Kit realised now that any hope must lie when they left the chaise, and could only hope that the boat might not already be waiting. There was, of course, the chance that Alicia would free the Major and that he, when informed by his batman of what had happened, would immediately set out in pursuit. Just how long it would take the Major to decide which way they had gone he preferred not to consider. He did not value his chances of escape once on board the French ship. Allowing half an hour for Alicia to bring the Major out of the tunnel—and this, he felt, was far longer than it must take—ten minutes for the batman to tell his master what happened, another ten to saddle the horses, and an hour to find them, it really was not worth straining his ears, as he realised he was, for sounds of pursuit.

It was nearly dark now. Peering from the window Kit knew that it would not be long before the shapes of bushes and trees passing by became merely dark shadows. At once the panic that had been rising gradually from his toes ever since he had found himself shut up with two such desperate men threatened to overcome him. How, in the pitch black of a clouded night, could two men expect to find one chaise? If they did not, how would he, hopeless creature that he was, succeed in stopping these two men before him, the one apparently asleep, and the other, whose cold eyes had never once closed, had hardly, in fact, flickered from Kit's face? For a wild moment Kit thought of seizing the pistol that lay so close beside him in the holster. Gregory had his eyes fast closed, so perhaps, if he were quick enough, he could pull it out and point it at them before they realised what was happening. The two of them. It was, indeed, a daunting prospect, but Kit came to the conclusion that he had been coward too long, and that the time had come for action. Besides, if he sat still much longer he felt he could not be certain of his control. Of course, he did not know if the weapon were loaded. How could he tell, he wondered, without actually cocking it and firing it? He risked a surreptitious glance at the weapon, and it was just this that Gerande had been waiting for. Kit was hardly aware of his having moved, but the next moment Gerande was sitting beside him on the seat, a dangerous glitter in his eyes, with a knife far slimmer, and more wicked-looking than Kit's own, pressed strategically against his throat. He could not move, could not even turn his head the better to see the Frenchman, but from the corner of his eye he could see a very unnerving expression indeed on that cold, hard face. Gregory, too, was awake. Had he ever been asleep? He had laid aside his smelling salts, and although he was certainly pallid there was something in the lines of his face that gave Kit no reassurance.

'So, my dear friend, you were right indeed! Christopher, dear coz, I am disappointed in you!' He spoke sadly, and shook his head. 'My friend and I, you see, partook of a little wager, of which, it seems, he is unfortunately the winner.' He sighed, and closed his eyes for a brief moment. 'Our friend, you see,' he continued, his expression pained, 'found, alas, that he could not trust you, could not believe, in truth, that you were sincerely dedicated to our cause. Loath as I was to credit this I decided on one final test which, dearest coz, you have failed. The pistol is unloaded.' He turned his pained expression on the Frenchman and said softly: 'I think, my friend, that the knife will not be necessary. You must see for yourself that you have reduced my poor relation to such a state of incorporate fear that he will be quite unable to move.'

For a moment it seemed as though Gerande had not heard. He remained seated with the knife pressed lightly against Kit's throat, so lightly, in fact, that he could hardly feel it, and then he moved, swiftly, to his original position in the carriage. Kit relaxed a little. With Gerande beside him it was true he had been too terrified to move, but much of this terror had been occasioned by the knowledge that an unexpected rut or furrow in the road would mean the end for him, whatever Gerande himself intended. Now he let breath out, and regarded his cousin silently, pale, but composed. The panic that so lately had threatened to take him had subsided. He felt, now that the crisis had arrived, he could do what was necessary.

There was mockery in his cousin's eyes as they regarded him from across the carriage. He had seen the fear so plainly, and Kit raised his chin a little.

'So, my dear cousin is not to be trusted,' murmured Gregory, the brown eyes derision-full. 'How long, I wonder, have you contemplated such treachery? Surely not always?' He put his head on one side and narrowed his eyes. 'No, for I should have known. Recently, then.' Enlightenment appeared to dawn, the thin lips smiled. 'Since my sweet Alicia spoke to him. She is a dream, indeed! And, sweetest Christopher, dear coz, she has persuaded you from your convictions! And you, at one time so convinced!' He shook his head, his eyes alive. 'What were you at, then I wonder? Did you intend to ensnare the two of us? Even *you*, coz, could not be so foolish as to attempt such folly!' He frowned suddenly, the dark brows snapping together across the bridge of his nose. 'Unless—' He stopped, glanced sharply at the motionless figure beside him. 'Perhaps we are to expect company. Can it be so, indeed? Has my ingenious little cousin contrived to rescue our dear Major?'

Kit said nothing, trying to keep his face, his eyes, expressionless. Both Kenyons turned, however, as the Frenchman spoke from the seclusion of his corner.

'There is nothing to fear,' he said, his eyes fixed unblinkingly on Kit's face. 'I have laid a charge.'

Expression flooded Kit's face now. Pallid already, all vestige of colour drained away as he stared across the darkening coach, sickening horror flooding him.

'A charge,' the Beau repeated thoughtfully. 'Can it be, my friend, that you have anticipated?'

The Frenchman flicked an irritated glance in the Beau's direction and said: 'I saw the girl. She went to save the soldier. So I laid the charge at the entrance. Neither can escape.'

All caution deserted Kit. 'Murderer!' he cried disregarding his cousin. 'In cold blood! How could you? That was my *sister*!'

'Indeed,' said the Beau thoughtfully, 'I am a little grieved myself. I had much rather, my friend, that you consulted me before taking such action.'

Gerande shrugged. 'I consult no one,' he said shortly.

The Beau seemed annoyed. 'That is apparent,' he replied, more sharply than was his wont. For a moment he did not continue, seemed to collect himself, and then said: 'However, perhaps it is best, after all. I own, I regret my cousin's passing, but then, we cannot allow such a thing as sentiment to intrude, can we, dear coz?' He eyed his cousin speculatively, but Kit, who no longer cared for anything, was huddled into the corner, shivering uncontrollably. The Beau looked thoughtful.

For a while Kit's mind refused simply to accept the facts. His head almost completely empty, he sat limply in the corner, swaying with the chaise, making no attempt to clutch at the leather strap that dangled beside him, content to be thrown violently against the side of the carriage when the wheels dropped unexpectedly into a rut. Gradually, however, the blankness of his mind began to clear, some of his native common sense taking over. Gerande could not know Alicia was dead. He had laid the charge, certainly, but there could be no way of telling whether it had achieved what was intended. With a great effort Kit forced himself to consider the tides, and did not find consolation in the fact that the cave would certainly be flooded and impassable, that escape that way would be impossible until the early hours of the morning. The chance that Alicia might yet be alive, however, could not be dismissed, and Kit, while maintaining his attitude of mindless imbecility, thrust aside the clouds in his brain and attempted to think clearly.

He had one cause for hope. If Gregory did not intend to kill him at once there was the chance that the batman, Chegg, might reach them in time. The possibility that he might decide to search for his master Kit did not consider seriously. Chegg had clearly been heading for the stables when Kit had seen him last, surely with the intention of pursuit. This recollection cheered the young man, and if he could only know that Alicia was safe he would be confident again. If she were dead, he would never forget that he had sent her to the tunnel.

At the moment, however, he knew his immediate concern must be for his own safety. The carriage had not faltered during the recent excitement, Gregory had made no attempt to bang on the roof and stop it.

Gerande, his eyes alert as usual, had returned to his seat. Both watched him, and said nothing. Thinking more dispassionately now than for several weeks Kit saw that it had all been a false hope. Herringham was irretrievable; he had been a fool. If the Major survived, how would he react when confronted by a young traitor? Surely it was his duty to turn him over for trial? Kit did not doubt that he would do so, and what the outcome of such a trial would be. He found he did not care about his own fate, but an anger, cold and frightening in its intensity even to him, gripped him suddenly and he made a promise to himself that even if it came from his own hand, Gerande would not escape Justice. Meanwhile it was necessary to preserve life. He drew his legs up onto the seat and curled his knees beneath his chin. Beneath the unblinking gaze of the two men opposite he lay huddled on the seat, gently rocking with the motion of the chaise.

# CHAPTER
# ELEVEN

WHEN Chegg and Lord Harbury left the Fox and Goose they walked straight into the first scudding shower of rain that would herald a wild night. The landlord had responded to his guests' sudden and wholly unexpected demand for horses readily enough, not even trying to understand a situation the exigence of which sent his notable patron back onto the road the instant he had sat down. Paul had not waited for explanations. No sooner had he gathered from Chegg that his brother lay bound and gagged in a chaise not ten minutes ahead of them than he had lost all desire for his supper, striding from the room with an urgency that surprised even Chegg.

He hardly noticed the rain. What he did notice was that it would remain light for barely half an hour, when their chances of following the chaise would be considerably lessened. This, at the moment, was all he cared about. His exhaustion, from travelling hard all day, fell away from him. He was alive again, refreshed, his energies renewed by the knowledge of Andy's whereabouts, by the need for action.

London had proved to be trying. Everywhere he turned was a dead end. His friends in the Government had either expressed no knowledge at all, or had told him simply to leave well alone. His visit to the Home Office had proved equally fruitless. Two days he had lingered, until finally, spurning idleness, he had decided on a journey to Sussex where was situated, he had been informed, the seat of the family Kenyon.

Just what he had expected to find he could not conjecture, and was more than half inclined to believe that his whole excursion was a waste of time and that nothing would be discovered. He was, moreover, anxious to be at home. Corinna's time was fast approaching, and although her confinement was not for several days he knew enough of these matters to be concerned at anything that caused delay in his return. Now, however, as he and Chegg cantered easily towards the cliff road Corinna was not in his thoughts. He had hoped that Chegg might be able to offer an explanation during the ride, but the strength of the swirling, changing wind, driving the rain full at them, made conversation impossible. The wind caught at the words, tearing them from their lips the moment they were spoken. As a consequence his imagination was working hard. He knew now that whatever business Andy was engaged upon it was certainly dangerous, and, he suspected, highly important also.

Chegg had elicited information from the ostler that a carriage had passed some moments before his own arrival, but had swung, contrary to his expectation, onto the cliff road, a rough narrow track that pursued a tortuous course over the cliffs to join the London road some five miles further on. The ostler had noticed it with puzzlement, for few people took that road, particularly when laden, as was this carriage, with some weight of baggage. Paul had frowned at the news. He could see no reason for taking the slower, more difficult route, unless, he thought coldly, they intended to dispose of some of their baggage into the sea. Lowering his head grimly at the thought of this Paul urged his mount onwards. Just what would happen when they finally caught up, Lord Harbury was unwilling to guess. He had only the vaguest picture of the scene in the coach, but it seemed likely that there would be at least three with whom they would need to contend.

The rain was now getting worse. The heavy clouds were making the sky prematurely dark, and the rain, driving full in their faces as they cantered onwards, made seeing difficult. The horses, too, hated it. Water streamed from their glowing, steaming necks, heads thrust forward, ears flattened. The exhaustion of the last two days came again on Paul. His legs ached as he pressed them against the animal's sides, urging it onwards. His back, too, was growing stiff, though he sat straight enough. His body wished for rest, for the comfort of a bed, for food most of all. The rain had soaked his caped great-coat long before. It now hung sodden from his shoulders, weighing him down. He glanced at Chegg. The light was fading fast, but the little batman's expression showed to be unusually grim. At once exhaustion left him again. If the man were so worried—and surely he must know, of all men—then there was indeed need for haste, no room for tiredness, hunger. As if sensing his mood his mount, a chestnut stallion, strong, with powerful quarters, pricked his ears gamely, and slightly lengthened his stride. They drew slightly away from Chegg; he had to urge the rapidly tiring mare to keep pace.

They were by this time high above the sea. The wind and rain obliterated all sound of it but in the fading light Paul could see the roughness of it as it broke white against the rocks below. There would be no chance, he thought, for anyone tossed over those cliffs. Silently they rode on, and now the cliffs began to dip again, so that the horses cantered easily downhill. Now Paul could hear the break of the sea above the wind.

With a sign to Chegg he reined in, and stood looking down at the fading panorama before him. He could see

now for some little distance, but there was no sign of the
chaise, either below them or further away on the cliffs.
He frowned as a new idea occurred to him. He turned to
his companion. 'Tell me, Chegg, could they be contemplating a sea voyage?'

Chegg considered him grimly. 'France, my lord? Ay,
'tis possible, though I own it hadn't occurred to me.' He
turned his grisled head seawards. 'Ah, but 'tis a rough
night! Will anyone beach in this?'

'I don't know,' Paul said, frowning. 'I thought a
moment ago that there was something out there, but it
was the merest shadow, a trick of the light.'

Chegg stared out to sea. In the fading light the water
showed tossing and restless, foaming horses white
against the blackness of the sea. 'If they're desperate,
my lord, God knows what they might not try! And
desperate that top-lofty Beau Kenyon might well be, it
seems to me! A devilish rum card he was, my lord, and
no mistake!'

'Hmm.' Paul was thoughtful. Finally he turned his
horse and they cantered again gently down the slope
towards sea-level.

Lying on the seat of the chaise Kit had not moved. The
road out of the village was in such bad order that he was
sorely jolted, and several times had to repress the impulse that urged him to throw out a hand to save himself.
He was conscious all the time of the silence opposite
him, of the fact that Gerande and his cousin were
watching him. The angle at which he was thrown and
their speed told him whether they were travelling up hill
or down. Consequently he felt able, with some accuracy,
to judge their position, and calculate just when they
would draw into the small cove where they would beach
the tiny boat. Consequently it was with some small

satisfaction that he sensed the pressure of the brake on the wheels, and heard an indistinct murmur from the man on the box to his team. And then they were stopped. With a creak of wheels and snorting horses the carriage came to a ragged halt, one wheel dipped so badly in a rut that the corner in which Kit lay was considerably lower. All his senses alert he yet made no sign, until a rough hand jerked him forcibly upright, and propelled him through the door into the mud. Choking, he pushed himself onto his elbows, feeling the wetness of the mud in his hair, the stinging in his eyes. Falling into it face down his coat and breeches were now wet and heavy, but he forced himself to remain on all fours, repressing the urge to wipe the mess from his eyes and mouth. In a moment, however, the hand returned, and he was hauled upright. Gerande – Kit knew Gregory would never stoop so low – was now supporting him under the elbow, and he was half dragged away from the coach towards the little bay just below them. With his eyes closed against the stinging mud Kit felt the slope falling away, and suddenly, with the exchange of grass for pebbles, knew they had gained the beach. Behind him came the sound of boxes being thrown from the roof of the carriage, and he heard his cousin's exclamation at the coachman's rough handling. Stumbling now among the pebbles he moved with great difficulty down the beach. Gerande was sparing no thought for his comfort, and several times he tripped, to be dragged carelessly to his feet again and hustled onwards. When finally Gerande stopped he dropped him onto the hard pebbles, and Kit felt his breath warm on his cheek as the Frenchman bent low towards him.

'You are a very foolish fellow, my friend, I have always thought it. A boy like you should not concern himself in the affairs of men. Do not mistake me.

Whatever your charming cousin says if you move from here I shall take the greatest pleasure in cutting your throat.'

Kit did not move. He made no sound, and after a moment or two heard Gerande crunch away from him up the beach. Carefully he drew forth his handkerchief and wiped the mud from his eyes.

It was very nearly dark. He was sitting on the beach about a dozen yards from the sea, and could see the breakers, large and foaming, as they rolled and crashed inwards, throwing the pebbles up the beach and dragging them back again. It seemed to Kit, dispassionately considering it, that even if the ship did come they would in all likelihood be wrecked before reaching France.

It was as this thought came to him that he caught the first intimation of a shape on the horizon. There was no light, merely a darkness of outline, gone as soon as he had seen it. The ship had come, then. The question was whether they would risk the men to send a boat ashore. He turned his face into the rain that was driving down the beach, and caught the flash and wink of a lantern, as someone near the carriage signalled briefly. Gerande, Kit supposed, since the Beau would hardly stoop to such a thing. He turned back seawards, looking for the answering flash. For several minutes he saw nothing, not even the dark shape of the ship on the horizon, and then, as the swell lifted it up, he saw the faintest glimmer of light, gone almost as soon as it was seen. Now he heard the crunching again behind him, and he turned to see a shape walking up the beach bearing a lighted lantern in each hand. Not moving, Kit watched as the figure passed at a little distance from him towards the rocks on one side of the cove. As Kit had supposed, he placed the lantern on the top of a rock, and then walked across to do a similar thing on the other side. The boat was certainly expected. Shivering now with cold, Kit stared straight out to sea, waiting for the distant plash of oars that would signal the approach of the boat.

Riding down the slope, Paul Harbury had seen the movement of lights beneath him. At almost the same instant he sensed Chegg reining in beside him, and together they watched as the lights moved up the beach. The coach that Paul had failed to see from the top of the hill, was now darkly visible below them. Paul could not like the situation, for the odds seemed heavily poised against them, and every moment increased them with the imminent arrival of men in a boat. He found the hard shape of his pistol beneath his coat somewhat reassuring, but wished he could be sure where his brother was before he took his chance. Beside him Chegg sighed and glanced in his direction. 'The coach, my lord, I'll wager.'

'Perhaps.' Lord Harbury was thoughtful. 'I wish I knew how many we must attend to!' He signed. 'Well, Chegg, we will attempt the coach first. Perchance we might deal with them one at a time.'

Chegg grunted, and the two kicked up their mounts. At a walk they proceeded down the hill, seeking out the scrubby bushes that lined the route, in order to conceal themselves in the last of the daylight. The rain had lessened momentarily, and through the gloom Paul suddenly thought he could see a hunched form upon the beach. He frowned sharply, but then the rain recommenced, and the form, motionless as it was, seemed merely to be a rock.

When they were within a hundred yards of the coach Paul reined in again, and at a sign from him the two men descended, wrapping the reins about the branches of bushes. The man who had carried the lanterns was returning now; they could dimly see a figure moving up the beach. In a moment or two it was joined by another, and sounds of conversation were wafted vaguely up the beach.

Paul nudged his companion and signified by a gesture what he wished. Chegg nodded shortly, and drawing forth a stout pistol set off with the stealth of a soldier towards the coach. For a moment Paul watched him and then he too started forward on a different line. Judging that the attentions of all would be concentrated on the possible arrival of a boat Paul moved stealthily forward. There was movement in the shadow of the chaise, and at that moment Paul thought he could hear something like the splash and dip of oars. The man heard it too, starting forward, and simultaneously Paul saw a second figure, hunched and stealthy, come from a clump of scrubby bushes to administer a blow that caused the man to fall backwards gently. Paul grinned. Quickly Chegg dragged the unfortunate coachman out of sight. A moment later Paul had joined him.

'Well done! How long will he be out of action?'

Chegg shrugged. 'Long enough, leastways, for your needs!'

'Good! Now, is there a groom?'

'That top-lofty valet, my lord, if I remembers aright! Travelling on the box, 'e was, an' mighty put out 'e'd be, too! It'll be a pleasure to me to plant him a facer, I can tell you!'

'Yes, but we must find him first, must we not! Come, Chegg, the chaise!'

With a grunt Chegg started forward, and, with a quick glance at the forms on the beach, wrenched open the door. There was a muffled exclamation. Paul, ascertaining that the figure was not his brother, lunged forward and grabbed a flailing piece of anatomy, a leg, it transpired, and pulled the unfortunate owner into the mud. The figure, gibbering in terror, lay prone, and Paul touched it lightly with the toe of his boot.

'Be quiet, or I'll instruct my man to cut your throat.'

The gibbering stopped abruptly and Chegg, who had been studying the figure with some intentness, declared suddenly: ''Tis that plaguey thatch-gallows, Collins! The Beau's man, my lord! You leave 'im to me!'

There was a whimper from the floor and Lord Harbury moved his foot again, murmuring: 'Hold your peace, my friend, or I shall let Chegg loose on you!' Silence ensuing once more Paul said quickly: 'Bind him, Chegg, and make haste about it. We have no time to lose.'

The victim trussed and bound to Chegg's satisfaction with his own linen, Paul grinned and then turned to more pressing matters, leaving the valet prone in the oozing mud. For even then sounds were audible from the beach. Someone had spotted the boat, running forward with a shout to the water's edge.

'Leave him!' Paul commanded, as Chegg seemed inclined to linger over his captive. 'They are come!'

At once Chegg, mindful of his duty, turned without reluctance and ran after his lordship.

Hunched against the wind and rain Kit too had seen the lurching form, and had heard the shout of relief from behind him. It was at this moment that he became aware of a hardness against his hip that had been causing him discomfort for some little time past. With a peculiar lurch he remembered the existence of his old, rusted knife. The Beau had run to the water's edge, but where was Gerande? He risked turning his head, and saw the Frenchman a little way behind him, intent upon the boat. He knew there was little chance of escape; his main concern now was that Gerande should not go free, should not gain the ship that would bear him to freedom and safety. Gently he eased his hand into his mud-encrusted coat, and clasped firmly the chipped, split hilt of his knife. The boat was now clearly visible, and as Kit watched a man jumped into the shallows. Behind him he sensed Gerande's approach, and drew forth his knife. The Frenchman hesitated for a brief moment, something in Kit's stillness stirring some instinct in his brain. Then he came on, stretching forward one hand.

'Come!' he commanded. 'It is time to go!' Kit did not move. 'Come!' Gerande said again. He glanced once at the Beau who was even now wading through the surf. 'Get up or they will not wait!' Still Kit made no response and Gerande, in exasperation, clasped him beneath the elbow. At that moment some native cunning, that which had made him excel, caused him to stop, and draw forth with his free hand his own stiletto. Kit, unable to see, but aware of Gerande's sharp intake of breath, lunged forward, and felt his blade meet the resistance of flesh. Gerande gasped; Kit, fighting nausea, released the hilt, and received Gerande's stiletto in his thigh. He screamed and collapsed. Behind him came a shout; confusion reigned, and a shot rang out. Gerande let out a breath, and fell heavily at his side. Someone ran past him up the beach, and another materialised against the dark sky. He drew breath. 'Gregory! He must not escape!' The man hesitated a moment longer, and then ran off.

The boat had come within fifty yards of the shore. Gregory, dimly aware of some calamity, had paused in the shallows. The sound of a shot, however, had driven whatever heroic tendency had stirred in him, and he plunged forward again. A man came to greet him, shouting something Gregory could not hear. Behind him now there was a splashing, and another shout. He ignored it, and something seared his earlobe with a burning fire. He stumbled forward, falling to his knees in the water. For a moment waves covered him, and then strong arms possessed him, dragging him upwards. Gasping and choking he encountered rough wood, and fell face-first into the watery bottom of the boat. Someone bundled his legs in behind him, and there came the creak of oars in the rowlocks. There was a shout, and a shot. The bows lurched horribly. Above him the two men rowed for the French vessel.

'Chegg!'

Lord Harbury was in the water now, shouting after the batman.

'Come, man, let him go!'

At last Chegg seemed to hear. In spite of the tossing waves the boat had drawn strongly from him, and he was now chest-deep in water. He turned, therefore, and was immediately knocked off his feet by a strong wave. Lord Harbury called again, but there was no sign of the batman. Then, as he was about to plunge forward himself a figure surfaced not ten feet from him. He saw the man strike out, and then a wave caught him again, bearing him shorewards a few feet before enveloping him. For an anguished moment Lord Harbury scoured the waves, and then Chegg appeared again, barely a yard away.

'Thank God! Give me your hand!'

Chegg did not resist. Lord Harbury clasped his hand firmly, pulling him upwards and from the waves. 'You fool, man! They would have killed you, if you did not drown!'

Chegg coughed. 'That traitor! My lord—!' He failed for a moment, swaying a little, and Paul delayed no longer. He wished his shoulder would allow him to carry the man, but contented himself with holding his head above water and dragging him shorewards. For the last few moments he had given no thought to the men on the beach. Now, as Chegg lay gasping he started forward to the two huddled forms. They lay together, motionless. As he approached one stirred, and raised a hand. 'Sir, whoever you are, my sister is in the gravest danger!'

Paul frowned. 'Your name sir!'

'Kenyon, but please hurry, my sister!'

'Kenyon! Where is Major Harbury!'

Kit groaned. 'With Alicia, in the tunnel! I pray you, make haste! I know not what has occurred!'

Paul considered quickly. 'Are you hurt? Can you ride?'

'I . . . I think so! Do but help me up!' He glanced at Gerande. 'Is he dead?'

'I sincerely trust he is. Who was he?'

'A French agent,' Kit answered listlessly. 'But let us be away! I can ride, I am sure!'

'Very well.' Paul turned to Chegg who had risen and now approached them. 'Are you well enough to stand guard, my dear fellow? I must beg your horse for Mr Kenyon. It seems we must make haste.'

'Aye, my lord, of course, but I must beg you to have a care!'

'I will, Chegg, do not concern yourself. I will send help as soon as I may.' Chegg nodded, and together they assisted Kit up the beach.

# CHAPTER
# TWELVE

FOR some little time after the last echo had died away
Alicia lay quite still. She realised afterwards that she
must have drifted several times into slumber, but at the
time she was not aware of this. A heavy weight had fallen
across her, effectively pinning her to the ground. She
tried to move, but except for the uncomfortable pulsing
in her throat she had no feeling. For a moment she knew
panic, and then forced herself to be calm. She took a
deep breath, and was instantly seized by a paroxysm of
coughing that wracked her body and made her aware of
various aches and pains about her. Above her the Major
had not moved. She wondered if he had injured himself
dreadfully in protecting her, and tried not to consider
what this might mean. She breathed deeply again and
tried to think rationally. She found herself unable to
judge how long she had lain there, and whether she
could expect Kit to find her. In her heart of hearts,
however, she knew she must not depend on him, and
tried not to think of what his own position might be at
that very moment. It seemed most important for her to
rouse the Major, if that were possible. She opened her
mouth again, another fit of coughing seized her, and at
that moment she became aware of movement above her.
She tried to cry out but was effectively choked by dust,
and besides, breathing was very painful. Above her she
could feel the expansion of the Major's rib cage, and of a
sudden realised how important it was to her that he

should be safe. Breathing slowly she made a sound into the wetness of his coat, and she heard the fall of loose stones as the Major moved again.

He had arched himself a little way above her. She found her mouth free of his coat, and cried out quickly, before he could fall back on her: 'Major Harbury! Andrew!'

He did not fall back on her. He seemed to be supporting his body-weight on his elbows, his forehead still resting on the earth. She coughed again, and was aware of stabbing pains in her chest as she breathed.

The convulsions in the form beneath him seemed to pull the Major back to consciousness. Alicia heard him drag air into the lungs, and then began coughing as she had, and crying out as he did so. He heaved himself up a little further, throwing off more rubble, and Alicia felt herself able to move.

The Major had collapsed again, but at her side, groaning and coughing alternately. Slowly, carefully, Alicia dragged herself onto her knees, groping before her to find where he had fallen. 'Major?' she said, tentatively, and then with greater urgency: 'Major!'

'I'm here,' he responded hoarsely. His breathing was very shallow, his breath coming in rasping gasps.

'You're hurt!' she exclaimed, forgetting instantly the various bruises she had just discovered.

'My ribs,' he gasped, painfully.

Alicia felt helpless. 'What can I do?'

Andrew gave a short laugh, checked immediately. 'Nothing! It will be all right, eventually.'

'But it sounds as though you're in agony!' she cried, reaching out a hand towards him in the darkness.

He gave a gasping laugh. 'I am!' he said, 'but there's nothing you can do.' He fell silent for a moment, and then said, his voice steadier: 'Give me your hand. I'm holding mine out to you.'

She inched forward, stretching her hand before her, and touched his arm. At once he grasped her hand tightly. Alicia found it greatly comforting.

'Now, can you stand up? Are you hurt?'

'No, no! I'm sure I am not!' She struggled upwards as she spoke, feeling him rise also, with an involuntary cry.

'Can you remember,' he said, his breath coming in short gasps, 'if there were candles in this room? We must—have light.'

She hung onto him, partly for comfort, partly because she knew that in this total blackness it would be hard to find him again if she let go. 'I don't know,' she answered desperately, trying to remember. 'I think so, yes—oh, I'm not sure! There was a table, and blankets too, which you should have. You're still so wet!'

She felt his smile. 'Well, I've no idea at all which way we're facing, have you? So I—suppose we just guess. Which way do you think? I'll leave first choice—to you.'

Alicia hesitated. She tried to go back over her immediate movements when she had reached out for the Major's hand. She knew, when the Major flung her to the ground, that she had been facing the passage that led to the steps. Major Harbury had jerked her away from the entrance. She made her decision, and took the Major's arm. Slowly they made their way forward, but were checked almost immediately by a fall of stone. Holding onto her hand the Major bent forward, feeling the stones before him. At last he sighed, and stood up.

'If it was that way we're unfortunate, I fear. Come on, we'll try this way.'

Tentatively the Major inched his way forward across the rubble of the floor, Alicia clinging firmly to him. They moved further this way, but once again a roof fall stopped them. To her consternation Andrew let go of her hand, but said, as though sensing her imminent panic: 'Take my coat. I shan't—leave you behind!' He leant forward onto the fall, feeling with his hands, trying to see how high it was. Alicia clutched the tails of his coat like a child at its nurse's skirts.

The Major was climbing slowly upwards. Pushing aside the fear that mounted in Alicia as he moved away from her, she started tentatively on the lowest stones, but her task was made harder by the loose stones sent down onto her as the Major climbed.

At last he turned and called down to her. 'Give me your hand, Miss Kenyon. The fall is only a small one.'

She stretched her hand forward in the darkness, moving it from side to side until she met his fingers. Then he began to haul her up across the untidily piled rocks and boulders, Alicia giving involuntary cries as she tripped or caught her foot in some unexpected obstacle. Once her foothold failed altogether and she went slithering back down, tearing her legs and face. The Major's grip was firm, however, though it almost pulled her arm from its socket, and she finally gained the top.

The fall was indeed small. They slithered comparatively easily down the other side and found themselves once more on firm ground. Then they began searching again, side by side, their free hands stretched out before them.

Alicia walked into the table. It was lying on its side, and the outstretched leg dug sharply into her thigh as she moved tentatively forward. She let out a cry which she checked immediately as she realised what she had discovered.

'It's the table, Major! The table is here!'

He was on his knees at once, groping with his hands for something recognisable. Alicia could hear his fingers running over a fine rubble of stones, and then she, too, dropped to her knees and began searching for that stub of candle she had convinced herself was here.

But it was the tinder-box she found. Searching desperately for the piece of wax she knew must be there, she almost overlooked the small hard object. It was only as she picked it up and felt it that she realised it was as valuable as the candle itself.

'Major,' she said, still stunned by her own nearstupidity, 'I've found something. It's a tinder-box.'

It was a moment before he replied, and when he did she could hear the smile in his voice. 'And I've found the candle.'

The light afforded by the single flame was negligible, but it was sufficient to make them aware of the devastation of the chamber, and of their own lucky escape. The way out was completely blocked by a heavy fall of stones. Elsewhere also the roof had collapsed. They themselves had been lying in one of the few safe places. For a moment both were silent as they surveyed what was left of the chamber. Alicia, as she contemplated their prison, felt an uprush of panic, and turned quickly to the Major. He was shivering violently. The panic subsided at once as she looked around quickly for the blankets. She found them after a moment, covered in a fine dust, in a pile where Gerande must have left them. There was a pillow too.

In spite of her protests the Major would only accept one. The other he gave to her, insisting that she needed it as much as he. 'We'd better get a fire alight,' he said, pulling the blanket closer under his chin, 'or we'll never survive the night.'

'And if we do survive, what then?' Alicia tried to sound unconcerned, but could not help the quiver from her voice.

'In a moment, when we're warmer, we'll have a look at the tunnel. We might be able to clear a way back to the cave.'

Alicia looked doubtful, but said merely: 'Should we burn this table, do you think? I cannot imagine anyone missing it!'

The Major grinned, and started to break up the table into more manageable pieces. It had been flung against the wall by the force of the blast and a crack had appeared down the centre. Andrew tossed it against the wall and it split at once, falling in two pieces to the floor. After that it was not so easy. The legs came away quickly enough, and the chair, too, was easily torn apart. After one or two more attempts to break the table the Major abandoned it.

Starting the fire was not easy either. Even the legs of the chair proved too thick, and Alicia was horrified when he suggested sacrificing one of the blankets. They sacrificed the pillow instead, pulling out the feathers and scattering them around the little pile of wood. They caught at once, and began to fill the cavern with a heavy, acrid smoke, bringing tears to the eyes of both. The ploy succeeded, however, and a pitiful little fire was begun on the floor of their prison.

Alicia felt ridiculously heartened as she watched the first tentative flame lick up around the shaped chair leg. It was such a small thing, but such an achievement, too. With warmth all things seemed possible.

When he was assured that the precious fire would not simply die away the Major, holding the blanket closely about him, moved to where the tunnel was, grimly surveying the devastation. The fall had been heavy. Many hours' work, he thought, would lie ahead of them. He glanced at Alicia. She was huddled over the fire, holding up the coat she had harried him into removing.

She was trying to dry it, a fruitless task, he thought, smiling ruefully, but a task nevertheless, and as such valuable. He turned back to the fall of rocks, peering upwards into the gloom. A vast hollow was above him from which the stone had fallen, and he realised that the rock could only be called dangerous. There was no way of knowing when another fall might take place.

A small sound behind him made him start. Alicia had draped the coat over a piece of table and had moved without him hearing her. She was standing behind him, staring with a grave expression at the task before them. He decided, looking at her, that the thought that it was futile could not be contemplated. She needed something to aim at if she were not to lie down and die. As for himself, he had known what it meant to despair, and would never do so again. The pain in his back had risen to a persistent scream; breathing was difficult—he could only take short shallow breaths without increasing the pain beyond toleration level—and yet he was able to ignore this when he looked at Alicia and saw the silent appeal in her eyes. He had not asked why she had betrayed him. He could guess, anyway, and would never, he decided, question her about it. He was content to take her as she was, whatever she had done, such was his love. If, one day, she chose to tell him, then that was her affair. He had not known he could love so completely, be so totally committed, that nothing could ever make a difference. He found it revealing and wondered if he could ever make her feel the same. He could not help believing that no one had loved quite as he loved, though his mind told him this was unreasonable. Paul, he knew, had loved in that way, his parents also. He decided his family had a great capacity for loving.

Alicia was looking at him with something of surprise, and he wondered what he had let her see. He did not

care. Turning back to his contemplation of the moun-
tainous task before him he said unemotionally: 'Could
you dry my coat, please? I can't wear this blanket and
work.'

She turned from him without a word and he realised,
too late, that she had wanted reassurance. He regretted
it, but turned back to the task before him. The thought
of removing a vast pile of rock with such agony in his
back was daunting. The smallest movement meant a
stabbing increase in pain, and he tried to concentrate his
mind on anything but his injury. He thought it fortunate
that Alicia could not feel his pain, or she would have
despaired indeed.

Slowly, peering upwards into the darkness, he began
to ascend the delicately poised pile, every faltering step
jarring the bones in his back. Once, when his foot
slipped on a loose stone, and he fell onto his face, he felt
the broken pieces of bone rub against each other. He
gritted his teeth, blotted his mind against the pain, and
moved on.

The fall proved higher than he had thought. A substantial amount had fallen from the roof, but the sides of
the tunnel had also collapsed, and the Major could not
help feeling that even if he succeeded in clearing a
passage for them they would be unlikely to escape
without a further fall impeding them. Lodging himself
on the topmost stones, his head a few inches from the
jagged ceiling, he began carefully to remove the upper
stones, rolling them down to the bottom.

The rattling down of the first stones brought Alicia
from the fire again to stand at a safe distance, staring up
at the figure she could barely see, but whose laboured
breathing she could hear plainly. She felt quite useless.
She knew he was hurt, and in great pain. Unknown to
himself he was uttering groans of effort with every

movement he made. She longed to be able to help him, even to tell him to let her do it, but with the knowledge of her betrayal so heavy on her the dread of rebuttal was large. She moved back to her former occupation of trying to dry the Major's coat. The fire was so feeble, however, and the coat so completely saturated, that it was quite futile; she barely succeeded in raising a thin trail of steam. With her mind on the Major she held his coat against the warmth, listening to the regular rattle-rattle of stones from across the chamber.

Alicia was nearly asleep when suddenly the noise was louder. She heard the Major give a sharp cry, and turned in time to see him half-run, half-slide from the pile of stones. At first she thought the ripple of stones that followed him had been caused by his precipitate descent, but then she realised, as it grew of a sudden both louder and heavier, that it was a new fall. She heard herself cry out, she knew not what, and saw the Major just escape the first thud of rock. Then, thunderously, the collapse of the tunnel began again, and all was obscured in a fog of dust. Instinctively she moved backwards, stumbling over their feeble fire, backing up against the wall. The candle fluttered and went out; the fire was smothered, and all dark.

Miraculously, Alicia was untouched. She stood against the wall, coughing painfully, one arm across her face to protect it from the dust. As before, the noise took a long time to die away. When at last she opened her eyes she thought the fire had incredibly not been put out. She peered through the swirling dust at the faint glimmer of light. Then her vision cleared and she could see the Major. He was standing across the chamber, looking at her. Shining down on his head was the first light of day.

# CHAPTER
# THIRTEEN

THE return to Herringham proved exacting. The knife
had not gone deeply into Kit's leg, but he was bleeding
steadily, despite the tight bandage Chegg had made of
Kit's neckcloth. The blood-loss had made him weak and
light-headed, needing to be helped into the saddle and
then falling heavily off the other side. Paul at this point
began to envisage difficulties. During the hours that
followed, Paul, anxious for his brother, was several
times tempted to ride on. Kit was holding the reins
loosely, his head bowed low over the animal's neck.
Although there were barely five miles to travel to Herringham Paul soon began to wonder if they would be
there before dawn, since it was almost impossible to see
the road. He was very conscious of the pounding waves
beneath him on one side, and turned to ask Kit if he
knew of some other way. It was a moment or two before
he understood why Kit gave no answer. He could hear
the horse snorting and shaking its head. It was only when
the animal moved close to him that he realised it was
riderless. Cold horror gripped him. The wind was strong
enough to have prevented his hearing the fall. How
likely was it that Kenyon had fallen over the cliff? He
gave himself a mental shake and told himself he was just
being fanciful. Accordingly he dismounted, and, one
horse on either side of him, set off back along the path.

After a long search—an hour or more, Paul vaguely
supposed—he finally came upon the hunched figure,

lying where it had fallen in the mud. One horse bent his head and snuffled at him gently. To Paul's relief Kit stirred and made a noise of irritation. 'Who is that?'

'Harbury,' Paul said, bending down. 'Can you walk?'

'I . . . I think so. I must have fallen asleep.' With an effort he dragged himself onto his knees, and then let out a cry of pure pain. 'My leg!'

'Lean on my arm. If I help you can you mount?'

'Where's the accursed horse? I can't see anything!'

'Give me your hand. Here, beside you!'

Fumbling for Paul's hand, Kit dragged himself upwards. With the return of his senses he recollected the need for urgency, and consequently gritted his teeth against the pain when Paul assisted him into the saddle. 'Let us be off!' he said, finding relief in irritability. 'Why do you delay?'

And then once more they were moving along the cliff top, Kit at Paul's side. All the time they could hear the pounding of the sea below them.

After another hour the rain that had so tormented them ceased and the wind dropped. There was a distinct lightening in the sky and Paul began to determine the dark shapes before them as distinct trees and bushes. Kit, too, began to look about him a little more, and finally exclaimed: 'That's the home farm, sir! We must be almost there!' So indeed it proved. And now, too, the perceptible lightening of the sky was seen not merely to be relief from the storm, but the coming of day. They had been riding for most of the night. By tacit agreement both men kicked up their mounts. It was not a time for idle conversation. Ignoring the gnawing hunger in his stomach and the persistent ache of the old wound in his shoulder Paul urged his mount onwards. Kit needed no urging to keep pace. Already guilt-ridden, the thought that Alicia might yet die because he had been too tired to reach her was too horrifying to contemplate and he pushed such an idea to the furthest corner of his mind. He felt very cold that morning. His clothes had been saturated the night before and were now beginning to dry on him. Periodic fits of shivering made control of his horse somewhat difficult, the animal being at a loss to interpret the occasional uncontrolled shudders and jerks from the man on his back. Kit wondered that his companion should seem so little affected by the conditions.

They reached Herringham within fifteen minutes. They did not dismount until they had ridden to the site of the old labourer's cottage. Kicking his feet free of the stirrups Kit almost fell from the saddle, landing awkwardly and crying out at the pain in his leg. The trembling in his arms and legs would hardly allow him to grasp hold of the iron ring and raise the trap door. What he saw cast him into despondency. It was clear at once that the passage was completely blocked. Kit stumbled down the steps to where the wall of stones barred his way, and began pulling helplessly at them, calling out his sister's name. Paul, who had followed him, tried to stop him, but Kit could no longer hear. In desperation, Paul twisted him round by the shoulder and delivered a stinging slap to the boy's face. For a moment Kit stared at Lord Harbury in bemusement and confusion, and then the blood rushed to his face and he turned his head away. In silence Paul contemplated the barrier between himself and his brother. The light in the passage was dim but he could see quite plainly that they had no hope of moving the stone. He turned away from the randomly-built wall, and at that moment the way out was darkened by two figures. He peered upwards, but the light was behind him, casting them into silhouette. Andrew and Alicia, however, could easily determine the two figures at the wall.

'It's my brother!' cried Alicia, gathering up her tattered skirts and running down the steps.

Andrew's reaction was more controlled. 'Aye, it is indeed, and I do believe, if my eye does not deceive me, that it is my brother too.'

Bed-rest was prescribed for Andrew Harbury. He made the obligatory protest, but it was plain to all that he was exceedingly glad to be closeted in his chamber and have all the arduous but necessary tasks undertaken by his brother. For two days he knew very little. The doctor gave him laudanum to kill the pain and a draught to help him sleep, and on the infrequent occasions when he regained consciousness he found himself watched over by benevolent and vaguely familiar faces. It seemed easier to sleep than to puzzle about it, so he obediently drank the liquid held to his lips and slipped once more into light sleep. When he woke properly he found his brother beside his bed. He found it oddly comforting, and managed a smile.

'Paul,' he said indistinctly. 'What the devil are you doing here?'

'I am running your estate, dear brother, as it happens, but I shall be exceedingly glad when you are in good order and able to take care of your own affairs!'

Andrew smiled sleepily. He lay in quiet contemplation of the ceiling for several minutes, but then a frown puckered his brow and he turned again to his brother. 'How long have I been asleep?' he asked suddenly.

'Two days, that's all. Nothing to worry about.'

'Two days!' Andrew echoed, attempting to sit up. He was prevented by an unexpected amount of padding at his waist, and sank back with a groan. 'Did that accursed doctor give me a draught? Damn you, Paul, I told you not to let him! There is so much to do!'

He tried to sit up again, but a stabbing pain caught him unawares, and he was not unrelieved to be pressed gently onto the pillows again. 'There is nothing at all for you to do,' said Paul calmly. 'In fact, everything is running very smoothly without you. I have employed a number of staff, but I daresay you will not mind that.'

Andrew grinned feebly. 'No, I daresay I shall not. But look here, Paul that's not what I was thinking about. There's that damned fellow Kenyon to deal with, and that accursed Frenchman as well.'

'Gerande is dead, Andy. I told you, but you probably forgot. I killed him on the beach, but it was Kit who brought him down.'

'Oh Lord! Kit! That wretched boy! He's poison to himself, Paul! I must do something for him!'

'Aye,' responded Paul feelingly. 'I've had the devil's own task preventing him from telling that contact everything! We found some very interesting papers on you, you know. It seems Gerande left them to incriminate you. However, it was he who had the copies, so your friend from the farm is vastly pleased on that score, at least. But the fellow insists on staying until he can see you. I told him young Kit was forced to assist his cousin because of a threat to his sister, and that he was taken as prisoner in the carriage, which, after all, is not far short of the truth.'

'Did he accept it?' Andrew asked sharply.

'I can't really say,' his brother answered frankly. 'That foolish boy is behaving in a way to cast doubt on any tale.'

Andrew frowned. 'The trouble is Gregory Kenyon will deny it!'

'He won't. He won't say anything at all.'

Andrew looked up. 'Dead?'

'No, gone to France. There was a boat, which he was

able to reach before we could stop him. Chegg nearly drowned trying to catch him.'

'Chegg? Is he all right?'

'Oh aye, well enough. His pride has suffered more, I think.'

'Poor Chegg,' Andrew said, sighing. 'I had rather caught Kenyon, but it's likely he'll be little welcomed in France, as a failure.'

Paul nodded, and after a moment's hesitation said: 'Miss Kenyon rather regrets his departure, I fear. She would much rather have seen justice done!'

Andrew chuckled. 'Would she, indeed! No doubt he spun her some deuced credible tale.'

'He did, but you helped him, you know, by letting Miss Kenyon believe you were a French agent!'

'She did not believe me, she believed nothing, not even that Father was a highwayman!'

Paul laughed. 'No small wonder at that!' His laugh died, and he grew serious again. 'You had better see her, Andy, if you are well enough. I think she feels her conduct could be misinterpreted.'

'I shall.'

Paul nodded and stood up. At the door he turned and said: 'I must leave you today, I fear. Corinna's time is near. In fact, I may already be overdue!'

The Major stared, and laughed. 'Congratulations! But do not let me detain you, Corinna would never forgive me.'

'She would, don't worry. Besides, I believe it is not a thing for fathers, and I should only fuss her. Mama will be enough. But I shall not delay, I think.'

'Do not! Paul, I feel guilty!'

Lord Harbury laughed, and left him.

Kit saw Lord Harbury leave. He had been hovering in the passage for some little time, and now, as he heard the door open he hopped back quickly into the doorway of his own room, and waited until Paul had gone. Then he walked awkwardly but calmly to the Major's doorway, rapped smartly and entered.

'Sir,' he said at once, beginning a well-rehearsed speech, 'I should like to explain—'

'Oh do sit down,' interrupted the Major, motioning him to a chair, 'you should not be standing on that leg. And there is really no need for you to go over all that bunkum for my sake, I daresay I know it quite as well as you. So let us hear no more about it.'

Kit blushed scarlet. 'Sir, you do not understand! I have betrayed my country!'

'If you say that I shall certainly send you for trial!' responded Andrew irritably. 'At least, I should make out my report with the blame squarely on your shoulders, and we shall see where that gets us!'

Kit raised his chin. 'I hope I am able to accept the judgement of my peers.'

Andrew smiled wearily. 'Oh, do cut line, Kenyon! Where do you get your phraseology? You would do better to speak out of turn occasionally than to prose on in that dashed dull fashion! It is my judgement you must accept, and be grateful for it.'

'Very well, Major,' said Kit, standing up awkwardly. 'How do you find me?'

Andrew regarded the gaunt, stiff-backed young man silently for a moment, and then a smile twitched his face. He controlled it immediately, however, saying: 'I find you a fool, Kenyon. You had no hope of saving Herringham. There was nothing anyone could do, and you were a fool even to listen to your cousin!'

Kit reddened uncomfortably. 'I know, but he said—'

'I care not for that. It is unimportant.' He fell silent and regarded Kit thoughtfully. 'What the devil am I to do with you?' he demanded suddenly.

'I hope you will hand me over to that representative of Authority at present beneath your roof.'

'Do you indeed! I wonder what your sister would say to that.'

Kit bridled. 'She is a woman, and women don't understand. I must ask you not to listen to her if she pleads for me.'

Andrew gave a bark of laughter. 'You will find, my friend, that they understand a great many things very well, although they do sometimes have their own way of looking at things. However,' and he grew serious, 'while you do not care for your sister's comfort I do, and it will not suit her to have a brother hanged for treason.'

Andrew watched him carefully, noticing that, although the boy was pale, he did not flinch at the Major's words. 'Nor,' he added thoughtfully, 'will it suit me.'

Kit looked puzzled. 'I don't understand. What concern of yours is it what suits my sister?'

Andrew smiled faintly. 'I hope to make it very much my concern, but how would I look to Miss Kenyon if I sent her dearest brother to the scaffold? Not very rosy, I fear me.'

Kit's brow cleared. 'You mean—? I say!' he exclaimed, momentarily diverted. 'That would be beyond all things great! I know Ally would love to be able to stay at Herringham, and—' He broke off, frowning again. 'Look here, that's not why you're doing it, is it? Because of the house?'

'Good God!' exclaimed Andrew irascibly. 'What a dashed odd notion you have of me! I hope I am not such a looby! I want to marry your sister because I love her, not from my misguided sense of duty because I happened to purchase her brother's house. Which I did perfectly legally, you will be pleased to hear.'

Kit flushed again, but said: 'I'm glad. But neverthe-less, my sister must be made to realise that what I did was wrong, and I must be punished for it!'

'You have been punished. Herringham is mine, and I am master. No Kenyon will ever call it his own again.'

The two men regarded each other gravely, and then Kit's eyes fell. 'To lose the house is more than anything. After that nothing can seem as bad.'

'Then let us hear no more about it,' Andrew said briskly. 'I shall make out my report, exonerating you, and that will be the end of the affair.'

Kit forced himself to look at the scarred face of the man before him. 'I suppose I must thank you,' he said, holding out his hand with a jerky movement, shaking the Major's curtly and letting it go.

Just then a soft knock fell on the door. 'Be a good fellow, Kit, and see who that is. If it's a draught I don't want it.'

It was Alicia, and she hesitated when she saw her brother. 'I'm sorry, it is unimportant.'

She turned to go, but the Major said hastily: 'No, stay, we are finished.'

Kit glanced from one to the other. 'Perhaps I ought to stay too,' he said.

'The devil take you, Kenyon! Get out!'

Kit looked startled, but then his expression cleared, and he controlled a grin. 'Oh, very well. Er, thank you, sir.'

'The young cub,' the Major said mildly as the door closed. 'He'll do well enough.'

'Will he?' said Alicia, coming forward with a look of anxiety. 'I know I shouldn't really ask you, but I suppose he must go for trial? There is nothing you can do?'

The Major regarded her from beneath his brows.

'What would you have me do?'

'Anything!' she cried impetuously. 'He is just a foolish boy, can't you see that? He thought he was doing it for the best!' She was at his side now, a look of earnest entreaty on her face.

'There are a great many men who have acted for the best, Miss Kenyon. He might have caused great harm.'

'But he did not! Oh please! Surely there is something you can do? I would be so grateful!'

His eye flickered. 'How grateful?'

'Very, very grateful,' she responded sincerely.

'Indeed! Perhaps I should give it some thought.' He frowned as though in concentration, but then, glancing at her drawn, worried features, his conscience smote him and he smiled. 'My love, I have already told him he will not be tried! Do not fear!'

As she looked at him, her heart full, she failed to notice the familiarity with which he addressed her. 'Thank you! Oh, I can never be grateful enough!' She stepped forward impulsively, and caught his hand as it lay on the counterpane. '*Thank* you,' she said again, tears in her eyes.

Her hand was held in a firm grip. As she tried to draw it away he grasped it the tighter, and the colour rose in her face. 'Major Harbury, this is hardly proper!'

'No more is it,' he agreed equably. 'In fact, a great deal of what we have done has been distinctly improper! Perhaps you have forgot that we were one full night in the tunnel?'

Her colour considerably heightened she tried to pull away her hand, but he held it firmly. 'If you were a gentleman, sir, you would not remind me of such a thing!'

He laughed. 'My sweet, have I not told you that I am no gentleman? Do you know me so little?'

'I know you as well as I intend to,' she countered, her eyes flashing.

'Oh, my love, my love, so angry! Will you not cry truce? After all, I have pardoned your Kit!'

His eye teased her, and emotions of anger and mortification arose within her. 'Sir,' she said, her voice throbbing. 'I did not think you could take my promise of gratitude in that way!'

'In what way, my love?' he inquired innocently, opening his eye wide.

'Oh!' she exclaimed, goaded. 'You . . . you . . . !' She hesitated, searching for the right word.

Meanwhile the Major, taking pity on her dilemma, pulled her down to him, and silenced her by kissing her very firmly.

At first she struggled, squeaking her protest beneath his embrace, but gradually she relaxed a little, waiting for him to release her. When he did she did not at once rise, but instead sat looking at him gravely, her hand still reposing within his. 'Major, what do you want of me?'

He laughed, and pulled one long curl affectionately. 'My love, do you doubt me? I have compromised you shamefully, have I not? What chance have you of marriage with a reputable man? I must do the honourable thing.'

'Thank you,' she responded stiffly, 'but I don't see the need for such extreme measures.'

'Alicia, my little fool, do you not see I love you?'

She looked at him now, and saw the truth of it in his face, his expression so intense she could barely breathe. 'But how can you?' she managed at last. 'I *betrayed* you! You could have been killed!'

'You saved me, too, my love,' he reminded her gently. 'Besides, there was never any doubt in my mind as to why you did what you did.'

'Never?' she asked, raising her eyes shyly.

'Never,' he responded, raising her fingers to his lips and kissing them.

'Then why didn't you say so!' she cried wretchedly. 'You must have known how terrible I felt! You could have told me!'

'Yes. I'm sorry, my love. Will you forgive me?'

She risked another look into his eye, and felt her heart behaving in a most peculiar way. 'Yes,' she said simply. 'I will.'

A few minutes later she removed herself from the Major's grasp, reminding him that he was still convalescent and should not be unduly excited. He laughed and winced.

'But Andrew,' she said thoughtfully, her hands in her lap. 'I am wondering about Kit. You did say once he might manage the estate for you. Have you asked him?'

He sighed, and lay back on his pillows. 'I was wondering how long Kit would be out of your thoughts. I had hoped it would be for longer. No, I haven't asked him yet. I doubt if it would have done any good, feeling as he did. I gave him a rare trimming, you should know, which is no more than he deserves. I'll ask him tomorrow, or the day after.'

'Thank you,' she said demurely, regarding him from beneath her lashes.

He smiled, and took her hand again.

'But what will you do?' she asked him. 'Will you stay here?'

'Well, I shall have to go to London in a couple of days to the Home Office. Then I shall return here.'

'You are going to live at Herringham?'

He nodded. 'I have much to learn, but I mean, with your brother's guidance, to make Herringham viable again. Will you help me?'

She blushed, and looked away.

'Alicia, I want you to marry me! And really, after the way you behaved just now you have very little choice!'

She blushed becomingly and laughed a little. 'Andrew, are you sure you want to marry me? I'm so ordinary! And penniless!'

The Major's answer was to grasp her firmly about her trim waist and pull her to him. And in a very few minutes Miss Alicia Kenyon had been convinced that the only course appropriate was for her to change her name to his.

# Masquerade
## Historical Romances

# Intrigue excitement romance

Don't miss
May's
other enthralling Historical Romance title

**THE DANGEROUS GODDESS**
*by Rose Hughes*
*"You're not like other women, my dangerous goddess. You're too beautiful. Men will rob for you, kill for you . . ."*

Bound for India to join her soldier fiancé, Miranda Coulson lightly dismisses this description by a fellow passenger. On arrival in Bombay she is met, not by her fiancé who has been drafted to the North-West Frontier, but by the sardonic Captain Adam Redmond, who brusquely tells her to take the next ship home. Exotic India of 1897 fascinates Miranda and a chance meeting with Prince Salim of Rhajipur intrigues her further. But ruthlessly the arrogant Prince abducts her to his Palace of the Golden Tiger where Miranda is forced to recall the fatal words – a dangerous goddess . . .

You can obtain this title today from your local paperback retailer

# One of the best things in life is …FREE

We're sure you have enjoyed this Mills & Boon romance. So we'd like you to know about the other titles we offer. A world of variety in romance. From the best authors in the world of romance.

The Mills & Boon Reader Service Catalogue lists all the romances that are currently in stock. So if there are any titles that you cannot obtain or have missed in the past, you can get the romances you want DELIVERED DIRECT to your home.

The Reader Service Catalogue is free. Simply send the coupon – or drop us a line asking for the catalogue.

Post to: Mills & Boon Reader Service, P.O. Box 236, Thornton Road, Croydon, Surrey CR9 3RU, England.

*Please note: READERS IN SOUTH AFRICA please write to: Mills & Boon Reader Service of Southern Africa, Private Bag X3010, Randburg 2125, S. Africa.

Please send me my FREE copy of the Mills & Boon Reader Service Catalogue.

NAME (Mrs/Miss) _____ EP1

ADDRESS _____

_____

COUNTY/COUNTRY _____ POST/ZIP CODE _____

BLOCK LETTERS, PLEASE

## Mills & Boon
the rose of romance